Jane Gardam has won two Whitbread awards (for *The Queen of the Tambourine* and *The Hollow Land*). She was also a runner-up for the Booker Prize (for *God on the Rocks*, which was made into a much-praised TV film). She is a winner of the David Higham Award and the Royal Society of Literature's Winifred Holtby Prize for her short stories about Jamaica, *Black Faces, White Faces*, and *The Pangs of Love*, another collection of short stories, won the Katherine Mansfield Award. *Going into a Dark House* won the Macmillan Silver Pen Award. In 1999 she was awarded the Heywood Hill Literary Prize for a lifetime's commitment to literature.

Jane Gardam was born in Coatham, North Yorkshire. She lives in a cottage on the Pennines and in East Kent, near the sea. She is married with three grown-up children.

GOING
into a
DARK HOUSE

....

Jane Gardam

ABACUS

An *Abacus* Book

First published in Great Britain by Sinclair Stevenson 1994
Published by Abacus 1995
This edition published by Abacus 1997
Reprinted 1998, 1999 (twice)

The stories in this collection appeared in the following publications:
'Blue Poppies', *Telling Stories*, Hodder & Stoughton, 1993
© 1993 Jane Gardam
'Chinese Funeral', *Best Short Stories*, Heinemann, 1990
© 1990 Jane Gardam
'The Damascus Plum', *The Compleat Imbiber* No. 16, Mitchell Beazley, 1992
© 1992 Jane Gardam
'Bevis', *Discovery* magazine, September, 1992
© 1992 Jane Gardam
'The Meeting House', *The Oldie*, December, 1993
© 1993 Jane Gardam

A CIP catalogue record for this book
is available from the British Library.

ISBN 0 349 10661 4

Printed and bound in Great Britain by Clays Ltd, St Ives plc

Abacus
A Division of
Little, Brown and Company (UK)
Brettenham House
Lancaster Place
London WC2E 7EN

For
Tim, Kim and Imogen

Contents

BLUE POPPIES

My mother died with her hand in the hand of the Duchess. We were at Clere in late summer. It was a Monday. Clere opens on Mondays and Tuesdays only. It is not a great house and the Duke likes silence. It offers only itself. 'No teas, no toilets!' I once heard a woman say on one of the few coaches that ever found its way there. 'It's not much, is it?' Clere stands blotchy and moulding and its doves look very white against its peeling portico. Grass in the cobbles. If you listen hard you can still hear a stable clock thinly strike the quarters.

Mother had been staying with me for a month, sometimes knowing me, sometimes looking interestedly in my direction as if she ought to. Paddling here, paddling there. Looking out of windows, saying brightly, 'Bored? Of course I'm not bored.' Once or twice when I took her breakfast in bed she thought I was a nurse. Once after tea she asked if she could play in the garden and then looked frightened.

Today was showery. She watched the rain and the clouds blowing.

'Would you like to go to Clere?'

'Now what is that?'

'You know. You've been there before. It's the place with the blue poppies.'

....

'Blue poppies?'

'You saw them last time.'

'*Meconopsi*?' she asked. 'I really ought to write letters.'

My mother was ninety-one and she wrote letters every day. She had done so since she was a girl. She wrote at last to a very short list of people. Her address book looked like a tycoon's diary. Negotiations completed. Whole pages crossed out. The more recent crossings–off were wavery.

We set out for the blue poppies and she wore a hat and gloves and surveyed the rainy world through the car window. Every now and then she opened her handbag to look at her pills or wondered aloud where her walking stick had gone.

'Back seat.'

'No,' she said, 'I like the front seat in a car. It was always manners to offer the front seat. It's the best seat, the front seat.'

'But the stick is on the back seat.'

'What stick is that?'

At Clere the rain had stopped, leaving the grass slippery and a silvery dampness hanging in the air. The Duchess was on the door, taking tickets. That is to say she was at the other side of a rickety trestle table working in a flower border. She was digging. On the table a black tin box stood open for small change and a few spotted postcards of the house were arranged beside some very poor specimens of plants for sale at exorbitant prices. The Duchess's corduroy behind rose beyond them. She straightened up and half turned to us, great gloved hands swinging, caked in earth.

4

The Duchess is no beauty. She has a beak of ivory and deep-sunken, hard blue eyes. Her hair is scant and colourless. There are ropes in her throat. Her face is weather-beaten and her haunches strong, for she has created the gardens at Clere almost alone. When she speaks, the voice of the razorbill is heard in the land.

The Duke. Oh, the poor Duke! We could see him under the portico seated alone at another rough table eating bread. There was a slab of processed cheese beside the bread and a small bottle of beer. He wore a shawl and his face was long and rueful. His near-side shoulder was raised at a defensive angle to the Duchess, as if to ward off blows. I saw the Duchess see me pity the neglected Duke as she said to us, 'Could you hold on? Just a moment?' and turning back to the flowerbed she began to tug at a great, leaden root.

My mother opened her bag and began to scrabble in it. 'Now, this is my treat.'

'There!' cried the Duchess, heaving the root aloft, shaking off soil, tossing it down. 'Two, is it?'

'*Choisia ternata*,' said my mother. 'One and a half.'

A pause.

'For the house, is it? Are you going round the house as well as the garden?'

'We really came just for the poppies,' I said, 'and it's two, please.'

'Oh, I should like to see the house,' said my mother. 'I saw the poppies when I stayed with Lilian last year.'

I blinked.

'Lilian thinks I can't remember,' my mother said to the Duchess. 'This time I should like to see the house. And I shall pay.'

'Two,' I signalled to the Duchess, smiling what I hoped would be a collaborative smile above my mother's head. I saw the Duchess think, 'A bully'.

'One and a half,' said my mother.

'Mother, I am over fifty. It is children who are half-price.'

'*And* senior citizens,' said my mother. 'And I am one of those as I'm sure Her Grace will believe. I can prove it if I can only find my card.'

'I'll trust you,' said the Duchess. Her eyes gleamed on my mother. Then her icicle-wax face cracked into a smile drawing the thin skin taut over her nose. 'I'm a Lilian, too,' she said and gave a little cackle that told me she thought me fortunate.

We walked about the ground floor of the house, though many corridors were barred, and small ivory labels hung on hooks on many doors. They said '*PRIVATE*' in beautifully painted copperplate. In the drawing room, where my mother felt a little dizzy – nothing to speak of – there was nowhere to sit down. All the sofas and chairs were roped off, even the ones with torn silk or stuffing sprouting out. We were the only visitors and there seemed to be nobody in attendance to see that we didn't steal the ornaments.

'Meissen, I'd think, dear,' said my mother, picking up a little porcelain box from a table. 'Darling, oughtn't we to get this valued?' On other tables stood photographs in silver frames. On walls hung portraits in carved and gilded frames. Here and there across the centuries shone out the Duchess's nose.

'Such a disadvantage,' said my mother, 'poor dear.

That photograph is a Lenare. He's made her very hazy. That was his secret, you know. The haze. He could make anybody look romantic. All the fat young lilies. It will be her engagement portrait.'

'I'm surprised her mother let her have it done.'

'Oh, she would have had to. It was very much the thing. Like getting confirmed. Well, with these people, more usual really than getting confirmed. She looks as though she'd have no truck with it. I agree. I think she seems a splendid woman, don't you?'

We walked out side by side and stood on the semi-circular marble floor of the porch, among the flaking columns. The Duke had gone. The small brown beer-bottle was on its side. Robins were pecking about among the crumbs of bread. The Duchess could be seen, still toiling in the shrubs. Mother watched her as I considered the wet and broken steps down from the portico and up again towards the gardens, and my fury at my mother's pleasure in the Duchess. I wondered if we might take the steps one by one, arm in arm, with the stick and a prayer. 'Who is that person over there digging in that flower-bed?' asked Mother, looking towards the Duchess. 'A gardener, I suppose. They often get women now. You know – I should like to have done that.'

Down and up the steps we went and over the swell of the grass slope. There was a flint arch into a rose garden and a long white seat under a *gloire de Dijon* rose. 'I think I'll sit,' said my mother.

'The seat's wet.'

'Never mind.'

'It's sopping.'

She sat and the wind blew and the rose shook drops
and petals on her. 'I'll just put up my umbrella.'

'You haven't an umbrella.'

'Don't be silly, dear, I have a beautiful umbrella. It was
Margaret's. I've had it for years. It's in the hall-stand.'

'Well, I can't go all the way home for it.'

'It's not in your home, dear. You haven't got a
hall-stand. It's in *my* home. I'm glad to say I still have a
home of my own.'

'Well, I'm not going there. It's a hundred miles. I'm not
going a hundred miles for your umbrella.'

'But of course not. I didn't bring an umbrella to *you*,
Lilian. Not on holiday. I told you when you collected me:
"There's no need for me to bring an umbrella because I can
always use one of yours." Lilian, this seat is very wet.'

'For heaven's sake then— Come with me to see the blue
poppies.'

The Duchess's face suddenly peered round the flint
arch and disappeared again.

'Lilian, such a very strange woman just looked into
this garden. Like a hawk.'

'Mother. I'm going to see the poppies. Are you
coming?'

'I saw them once before. I'm sure I did. They're very
nice, but I think I'll just sit.'

'Nice!'

'Yes, *nice*, dear. *Nice*. You know I can't enthuse like
you can. I'm not very imaginative. I never have been.'

'That is true.'

'They always remind me of Cadbury's chocolates, but
I can never remember why.'

I thought, 'senile'. I must have said it.

I did say it.

'Well, yes. I dare say I am. Who is this woman approaching with a cushion? How very kind. Yes, I would like a cushion. My daughter forgot the umbrella. How thoughtful. She's *clever*, you see. She went to a university. Very clever, and *imaginative*, too. She insisted on coming all this way – such a wet day and, of course, most of your garden is over – because of the blue of the poppies. Children are so funny, aren't they?'

'I never quite see why everybody gets so worked up about the blue,' said the Duchess.

'*Meconopsis Baileyii*,' said my mother.

'Yes.'

'*Benicifolia*.'

'Give me *Campanula carpatica*,' said the Duchess.

'Ah! Or *Gentiana verna angulosa*,' said my mother. 'We sound as if we're saying our prayers.'

The two of them looked at me. My mother regarded me with kindly attention, as if I were a pleasant acquaintance she would like to think well of. 'You go off,' said the Duchess. 'I'll stay here. Take your time.'

As I went I heard my mother say, 'She's just like her father of course. You have to understand her; she hasn't much time for old people. And, of course, she is *no* gardener.'

When I came back – and they were: they were just like Cadbury's chocolate papers crumpled up under the tall black trees in a sweep, the exact colour, lying about among their pale hairy leaves in the muddy earth, raindrops scattering them with a papery noise – when I came back, the Duchess was holding my mother's hand and looking closely at her face. She said, 'Quick. You must telephone. In the study. Left of the portico. Says "Private" on a disc. *Run!*' She let go the hand, which fell loose. Loose and finished. The Duchess seemed to be smiling. A smile that stretched the narrow face and stretched the lines sharper round her eyes. It was more a sneer than a smile. I saw she was sneering with pain. I said, 'My mother is dead.' She said, 'Quick. Run. Be quick.'

I ran. Ran down the slope, over the porch, and into the study, where the telephone was old and black and lumpen and the dial flopped and rattled. All done, I ran out again and stood at the top of the steps looking up the grassy slope. We were clamped in time. Round the corner of the house came the Duke in a wheelchair pushed by a woman in a dark-blue dress. She had bottle legs. The two of them looked at me with suspicion. The Duke said, 'Phyllis?' to the woman and continued to stare. 'Yes?' asked the woman. 'Yes? What is it? Do you want something?' I thought, 'I want this last day again.'

I walked up the slope to the rose garden, where the Duchess sat looking over the view. She said, 'Now she has died.'

She seemed to be grieving. I knew though that my mother had not been dead when I ran for the telephone, and if it had been the Duchess who had run for the telephone I would have been with my mother when she died. So then I hated the Duchess and all her works.

It was two years later that I came face to face with her

again, at a luncheon party given in aid of the preservation of trees, and quite the other side of the country. There were the usual people – some eccentrics, some gushers, some hard-grained, valiant fund-raisers. No village people. The rich. All elderly. All, even the younger ones, belonging to what my children called 'the old world'. They had something of the ways of my mother's generation. But none of them was my mother.

The Duchess was over in a corner, standing by herself and eating hugely, her plate up near her mouth, her fork working away, her eyes swivelling frostily about. She saw me at once and went on staring as she ate. I knew she meant that I should go across to her.

I had written a letter of thanks of course and she had not only replied adequately – an old thick cream card inside a thick cream envelope and an indecipherable signature – but she had sent flowers to the funeral. And that had ended it.

I watched with interest as the Duchess cut herself a good half-pound of cheese and put it in her pocket. Going to a side-table she opened her handbag and began to sweep fruit into it. Three apples and two bananas disappeared, and the people around her looked away. As she reached the door she looked across at me. She did not exactly hesitate, but there was something.

Then she left the house.

But in the car park, there she was in a filthy car, eating one of the bananas. Still staring ahead, she wound down a window and I went towards her.

She said, 'Perhaps I ought to have told you. Your mother said to me, "Goodbye, Lilian dear." '

'Your name is Lilian,' I said. 'She was quite capable of calling *you* Lilian. She had taken a liking to you. Which she never did to me.'

'No, no. She meant you,' said the Duchess. 'She said, "I'm sorry, darling, not to have gone with you to the poppies." '

CHINESE FUNERAL

'I could do without the coffin,' said the Englishwoman. 'Going to China with a coffin.'

'It won't be here for long,' said her husband. 'They're taking it off at Lamma Island. We call in there. He's going to be buried at home. We're dropping him off. He died in Hong Kong.'

'How do you know it all?'

'Oh. I do. What's the matter with you? Coffins go all over the place. Aeroplanes. Ships. Cruise ships are full of them – empties for emergencies. I saw three in a stack once at Victoria Station. In Spain they arrange them round the undertakers' offices. On shelves. I've seen them. Wrapped in plastic, like long chocolates.'

'Oh, for heaven's sake,' she said. 'Anyway, those aren't full ones. This is a full one.'

'*They* were full,' he said, 'in Spain. No two ways.'

'Glib. Silly,' she said.

'Anyway,' said the husband, 'this one's out of sight. Below deck. You wouldn't know it was there if you hadn't seen it coming on board.'

'I can see the awful people,' she said.

Near the stern of the boat noisy men with excited eyes pushed each other about like lads on a treat. They wore sacking robes and their heads and hands were covered by slaphappy, bloodstained bandages, loose and trailing. The blood was not blood but vermilion paint. One man held a long trumpet. All had bare feet.

The husband said, 'I wonder if they're professional mourners.'

She said, 'It's awful. They're enjoying it.'

'Yes,' he said. 'A bit wild. The afterlife for them is horrible, you know. "The sleep of oblivion". Desolate. Frightening.'

'They're *enjoying* being frightened,' she said. 'They're getting a kick.'

'Yes and no,' said the husband. 'Yes and no. Don't forget they're surrounded by spirits.'

'Brandy.'

'No. Evil spirits. The trumpet is to frighten them away. Hong Kong isn't all computerspeak and banking. Well, Lamma Island isn't, anyway. Superstition goes deep.'

'It does with me, too,' she said. 'There's something about travelling with a coffin.'

'I'm surprised at you, Ann.'

'Not bad luck exactly,' she said. 'I don't know. Inopportune. Time rolling on. And back.'

'Well, so it does,' he said.

When the boat came alongside the sunny island he watched the waiting crowd of mourners on the quay and the bandaged people shouldering the coffin and bearing it away to the sound of the trumpet. The woman stayed in her seat reading the guidebook, her hands over her ears.

Fourteen were going on the day trip to China from Hong Kong. One was Nigerian, the rest British, all

unknown to each other. They had met on the Star Ferry
waterfront, Kowloon side, before dawn. They were all
middle-aged to old, a rather heavy, thoughtful lot, too
early awake. As the sun rose and they headed north to the
southern tip of China, threading the islands that lay in
strings like the humps of sea monsters ('It's where they
got the idea of dragons,' said the husband), the Nigerian
began to read a copy of *Time* magazine and the others
clicked about with cameras. One big old Englishman
straightened his shoulders and tightly blinked his eyes as
they stepped from the boat on to true Chinese soil. His
wife took his hand and they interlaced their fingers. They
stood looking at nothing in particular.

At the Customs, a woman in khaki, watching a screen,
stretched for Ann's handbag and removed from it two
apples that must have shown up on the X-ray. 'I suppose
they looked like hand grenades,' said Ann. The unpainted
mask-face did not smile but the eyes of soldiers standing by
looked sharp. 'I didn't know we couldn't bring them in,'
she said. 'Here – we'll eat them. It's a shame to waste them.'

But there was a sudden great fluster and the apples
were seized back from her hand and thrown in a bucket
where there were other wicked things – packets of
sweets, sandwiches in foil and a bottle of something. 'I
hope they get a pain,' said Ann. 'I suppose they'll eat
them the minute we're out of sight.'

'That we do not enquire,' said a voice. Standing by the
minibus that was to be their home till nightfall was the
Chinese guide, brilliant-eyed, happy, young. He ran
about laughing and shaking hands with the English
group. 'Here you leave Hong Kong behind and give

yourselves to me and to our driver here. He is a wonderful driver though he speaks and understands no English. He is my friend. I am a student of a Chinese university and he is uneducated, but he is my friend. For several years now, together in my vacations, we have guided Western tourists. We ask you to be patient with us. I ask you to ask me any questions you wish. I will answer everything. *Everything*. But we have much to do and far to go and when I say, "Come, hurry up please, no longer", you must obey. Thank you and get in.'

The driver had a long, unsmiling face. A precise and perfect line ran from eyesocket to the point of the jaw. A leaf. A Picasso. His white hands for the moment lay loose on the wheel. The hands of Moiseiwitsch. The guide was jolly, square-faced, amiable, with shaggy, fetching hair. Side by side the two heads turned to the road, giving it all attention. Ann suddenly saw the driver's hands running with blood and the guide with upflung arms, facing the dark. She cried out.

'What's the matter?' asked the husband. '*What* did you say? You're shivering. Put your sweater on.'

'It's—'

'Whatever is it? You look awful. Oh Lord, are you carsick? The road's going to get much worse than this.'

'No, I saw something. I don't know what— Something—'

'Will you forget that coffin!'

'No. Not the coffin. Something coming. Rolling like a sea.'

'They'll give us some tea soon,' he said. 'When we stop to see the kindergarten show and the market.'

18

'We got up too soon,' he said in a moment, and put an arm round her.

At the kindergarten show the human marionettes danced and sang and tipped their perfect little heads from side to side. Afterwards they ran across to the audience to shake every hand, a fixed smile on each blank-eyed face. 'Come now,' called the guide with his different smile. 'We have much to see and a hundred miles before lunch.'

'I'll find some tea,' said Ann's husband. 'There's always tea.' She stood waiting, watching the children being marshalled together for the next performance as a new load of tourists came streaming in. 'Could I see some of the ordinary children?' she asked, but the guide said, 'No, no, no – come.'

She sat in the bus, drank tea, felt better. Soon she began to watch the endless fields on either side of the road. Endless, endless. Grey. The thin crops, the frail, earth-coloured houses, here and there a pencilled, fine-leaved tree and a matchstick-figure in a round hat, scratching and chopping at the dun earth with a hoe. Chop and drag. Chop and drag. For hours they drove under a rainy sky. 'Time is over,' she said.

'Better?'

'Yes. I don't know what it was. It must have been a dream. It was a sort of – day-mare.'

'It was a short night,' he said 'You're tired.'

As the country faded by she began to see beauty in the timelessness and silence and hugeness of the land, the people scarcely touched down on it, like specks. At a lay-by, worn by other tourists' feet, they all got out to take photographs of peasants sowing seed on the plain. One ancient leather face looked up into Ann's camera. Looked away.

'Come now, come,' laughed the young guide. 'The road soon changes. It will become bad. After lunch it may be slow. We are going to a beautiful place for lunch. Well, it is the only place. Here it comes. It is perfectly hygienic. Do not judge by its surroundings.'

They picked their way through filth to the one new building in a sad town. Driver and guide disappeared and the party, spinning a turntable of food at two round dining tables, loosened up a little. The old Englishman ate sparingly, expert with chopsticks, the rest hungrily with spoons. The Nigerian ate hardly at all. All the food was pale brown. 'Not exactly Hong Kong,' said Ann's husband.

'It is *amazingly* good. Amazing,' said the old Englishman. 'Amazing that they can do this. You have no idea.'

'You know China?'

'Oh, yes. For twenty years. We lived here for twenty years and we left twenty years ago.' He looked at his wife who had no need to look back at him. '*And*,' he said, 'we are unlikely to be here again.'

'Oh – don't say that,' said Ann.

'Not because of our age,' he said. 'None of us may come back again.'

The guide reappeared. 'And now we shall hurry on,' he said. They noticed under the high electric bulbs of the echoing restaurant that he was rather older than they had thought and that some of the earlier insouciance was gone. Some of the acting. 'I shall warn you,' he said, 'we come soon to a point where it is not impossible that we must turn back. Before we get to the city there is often a huge traffic condition and we stand still a long time. It is known as the Rush Hour. A misnomer. I ask you to be patient if this happens and perhaps read books or sleep. Ask me questions or we perhaps might sing? May I ask you now at this moment not to look out to the left of the bus, please? Look only straight ahead, please, or to the *right*.'

Everyone at once looked out to the left, where a bedraggled and very long string of people dressed in white was moving at an urgent jog-trot over the fields towards the main road. Some wore tall white dunce's caps. All had fluttering streamers and dabs of vermilion paint. Four shouldered a skimpy coffin.

'To the right. To the right,' called the guide, 'the *right*. It is a Chinese funeral. Funerals are very important in China. It is not polite to watch them. In East or West it is considered ill-mannered to watch people's grief. It is not civilised to watch a Chinese funeral.'

'It is bad luck to watch a Chinese funeral,' said the big old Englishman into Ann's ear: he sat behind her. 'He is being kind to us.'

'It is our second today,' said Ann.

The driver put his foot down and they sped on, over a road full of holes and lakes of rain, past a sugarbeet factory red with rust. 'The Russians flogged to us that factory,' the guide announced over his microphone – his lunch and the funeral had excited him. 'The Russians made mugs of us. As usual. Nothing works.'

On they sped, past stagnant black water, ditches crammed with lotus leaves. A village. A temple. A

snowstorm of white ducks waiting to be cooked. In a
dirty town, pavement-artists gathered round the bus in
front of a defunct, red-lacquered palace, calling and
laughing. 'These are all students,' said the guide. 'These
are my tribe. Though they do not speak such good
English as I do. I am very good.' He laughed at himself
and the bus laughed with him and said he was telling the
truth. Someone began to clap. The Nigerian looked out
of the window. They flew on, rounded a bend and hit the
traffic.

It stood ahead of them as far as they could see. 'And
this,' said the guide, 'is where we must put to the test the
capacity for patience. At first I suggest we take some
sleep.'

Guide and driver, expert as grasshoppers, folded
themselves in their seats and a little of the black cap of
hair on each head, one polished, one shaggy, showed
above the ramshackle headrests. The heads leaned
together, like babes-in-the-wood. Ann felt her hands
ache to stretch and caress.

Again she felt a darkness round the two young men
and, turning quickly, frightened, said to the old Englishwoman, 'This can't be much fun for you. This new
China. Having lived here before. We thought it was all
supposed to be so much better now. Is it just that we've
been in Hong Kong for a week? Is it cloud-cuckoo?'

The Englishman said, 'Oh, no. It is wonderful to be
back.'

'Ha,' said the guide, bobbing up, arranging himself on
a perch by the dashboard, taking up the mike. 'This it
seems is a good opportunity. The driver does not speak

English and is in any case asleep. None of you will stay in China for more than a day. It is safe to tell you this then. China now looks forward with hope and joy. There is to be a great and glorious transformation. Blood will flow, but we stand to overthrow evil men and we shall win liberty. I ask you to think of me soon. At the time when the world will be watching us. You will remember me and what I say.'

Tottering as the bus jerked forward again, he fell aslant back in to his seat and turned away from them. For perhaps a mile they bowled easily along.

But then – round the next bend – they met the traffic again before them, ramshackle, dead-still, solid; and more came swinging up behind them, hemming them in tight.

'We shall now miss our train to Hong Kong from the city,' said the Nigerian, speaking for the first time.

'There is nothing to be done,' said the old Englishman, and settled back comfortably. His wife smiled.

Ann's husband said, 'Better sleep, Ann. We don't know what the end of this is going to be.'

'No.'

'Don't look so *doom-laden,*' he said. 'It's all education. After all, it's not our country – it has nothing to do with us.'

He hoped that she had not seen that the funeral party of an hour ago had caught up with them and was jogging along the side of the bus between it and the oily ditch of lotuses. The mourners' feet were black with dust, faces were hidden by white hoods. The crazed tall hats bobbed up and down as they passed by, and out of sight.

Zoo-Zoo

Sister Alfege was dying in the back of the Morris Traveller. She was dying no faster than last week or the week before that, but faster than the week before that, the month before that. She reclined in a sloped metal wheelchair, her back to the driver (who was Sister Luke) and the passenger (Sister Reparatrice): two faces forward, one face back; three black veils bulged together in a rusty clump in the centre of the car.

The blossoming Kent countryside flew past Sister Alfege on either side of her long black blinkers and dwindled away at speed before her so that she looked always at what had already passed and not towards what was to come, which caused her, somewhere much within, uneasiness.

She was so old, Sister Alfege. She had been at the convent half a century, since before the war, and she had been forty then. She was German, arrived in the 1930s from Hamburg with several other nuns. German nuns had been prospecting in foreign countries for several years, most of them choosing faraway accommodation in the Americas. The tiny English convent in Kent had welcomed a clutch of them and they had settled there with their devotional books, Latin down one side of the page, German the other. There had been a few whispers about spies and coded messages at first, until it was found that they had no electricity, never left the convent, never heard the news or looked at a newspaper. It hadn't seemed much of a sanctuary really, for the coast of occupied France could be easily made out from the kitchen garden and they could often hear the German guns.

Yet it had held up and they had survived. Many German nuns of course stayed in Germany and Sister Alfege had very much wished she could have been one of them. She had loved her country and her people and had wept for them. She felt herself to be God's, but very German, and of England she new nothing except the language, which she had learned as a small child at a good village school. Later she had been a teacher of English in a girls' school near Bremen, a rounded smiling woman pattering up and down the rows making everyone recite English poetry without looking down at their books. She had been respected, her wire glasses had flashed. She had missed nothing. Nobody looked left, right or out of the window as Sister Alfege paced about. Still she sometimes thought of the big toothy girls with their fat blonde plaits and pink print dresses and wondered how many of them had remembered 'The Wreck of the Deutschland' as the English bombs fell on them, and if it had done them any good.

Had she asked more determinedly to stay behind, would the Abbess Henrietta Friedeberg have let her? She had never asked, for although she had always looked so benignly soft when she removed her glasses Sister Alfege had found obedience her stumbling block since childhood. Her mother had tried to beat it into her to no avail and it had taken years as a nun before she could feel the least enthusiasm for it. So when she had been chosen to be one of those to leave Germany, she had left. It was her triumph of obedience. She held on to it.

And thus she had found herself living on the silt flats of East Kent in a long-neglected semi-ruin of a convent that nearly a thousand years before had been the headquarters of another German sisterhood, the abbey church of the Saxon St Esterbin of Bremen, a fearsome woman and first-rate accountant before whom merchants and politicians and bishops quailed. She had run a shipping line up and down the estuary of the River Thames and her laden barges had passed daily and successfully through the dangerous sandy channels beyond the abbey walls, manoeuvring themselves out into the open sea and back again. The abbey had flourished.

With Henry VIII had come the start of a few hundred years of emptiness – birds' nests, gaping roofs, lichens, cattle sheds, the pillaging of stone – until in the nineteenth century English nuns began nosing around again and talking of re-establishment. With the vigorous Germans of the early 1930s came new living quarters, a chapel and a rest-house for local ladies in Retreat. This last faltered in the war years beneath the screaming aeroplanes, but still the nuns stayed, the Germans watching the dogfights above them, the black swastikas and the red-and-blue bull's-eyes, first one plane and then another twirling down into the sea.

After the war Sister Alfege had returned briefly to Germany. She had done away with her glasses altogether now and looked vague, almost simple, and her Mother Superior found her much changed. A dreamy woman. Not at all the stuff for the desperate new Germany. The hard-won obedience was not noticeable either, for the first thing Sister Alfege asked was that she might return to Kent.

The abbess thought about it, sensed trouble, and agreed. They prayed together the night before Alfege left and in the morning Alfege walked alone to the boat with nobody to say goodbye to her. She never went back to Germany.

She had returned to Kent on a steely sea. At Dover she had taken the slow train – there is still no other – to Ramsgate. At Ramsgate she had waited an hour on a drenched promenade for the bus that was to jolt her over what had been in St Esterbin's time a lively causeway above running tides, now the graveyard of old airfields and plains of newly planted cabbage. The long wind-breaks of the poplars, unpruned for years, had more than survived the war and their corners rose far above the little bus, towering in a wondrous geometry like the prows of liners over a tug. In the fields around, crowds of seagulls were following tractors that carved long waves of milk-chocolate mud. From a white sky swishing rain had begun to fall. All colour died.

Sister Alfege had walked the last miles to the convent in her black blocky shoes carrying her small suitcase with the strap tied round it (the suitcase was beside her in the Morris Traveller now), her nose and fingers bright blue in the spring weather. In the suitcase had been her underclothing, her night shift, her Missal and a length of leathery German sausage, all rose-red and white within, more beautiful than icons in 1945.

She had opened the studded door to the once again scruffy courtyard of the convent and stepped inside as the fourteen threadbare sisters (there were only seven now) were lining up in the vestibule for vespers.

Over the years Sister Alfege had been unable to forget the sausage, which had disappeared, probably thrown to the pigs by the English nun who was then the cook and would never have seen such a thing before. If so, said Sister Alfege, it was a cannibal act and almost sacrilege. So much of her Germanness to the end of her life she retained.

The image, the metaphor of the sausage, returned to her now on the way to the Hospice of the Holy Rood. The sausage, the sudden violent paradigm of worlds renounced, the secret, marbled meat glistening with delicious fat inside the never-severed skin. Dying away in the Traveller fifty years on, her ragged old mind began alternately to shine and fade at the thought of it; and with other images: old ones from the Germany of her childhood and the immediate passing images flying by through the lanes, through Wickhambreux and Fording-bridge and Ash. The life between was gone.

Blossoms thrown like faint snowfalls across hedges of blackthorn rushed by so fast she could not think whether this was Kent or Luneberge Heide, where she had walked behind her father's cows with a stick through the furze, kept home from school when farm work was to be done. Then as now she had worn a long black dress but then as not now her hair had gleamed in silver-gilt ropes down her back. A white-headed child. She saw herself again (Sister Luke flung the car manically round Littlebourne corner: she drove seldom and the car was very old) and the haunches of the cattle still teetered above ten-year-old Sister Alfege's head like the hips of loose girls. The haunches had always been caked with mud – the farm had been lackadaisical – cracked like baked biscuit. Now and then the cows had flexed the muscle at the top of the tail and dropped out gold-green slops, and she had stepped round them in her wooden shoes. She could smell the steaming, wet, painty-looking stuff even now, sharp and lively. They had been used to tell her to breathe it in, deep down. It would strengthen her chest.

Sister Luke flung them round the next bend and was off down a narrow lane, a long lacy float of trees on one side, a high fence on the other. The trees were scarcely in leaf yet and through their lowest branches Sister Alfege could see hundreds of apple trees arranged like fairy soldiers, like pegs, stuck in a mesh of green pathways and every tree covered in hard knobs, sealing-wax beads. Next week they would be acre on acre of rosy blossom.

Now came the wires of the hop fields, tall harps for Titans. More hedges, more green shoots, red shoots, busy, ordered, industrious landscape. Teutonic. No. But not exactly English either. Maybe French? Sister Alfege had never thought anything of the French and shivered suddenly, feeling far from home.

But no. It's England of course. I dare say. I know it well. My eyes are good. The mind less so. It follows after.

She could not reach to dab, and so sniffed loudly.

The car careered up the side of the bank as towards them down the narrow road came a machine like a factory. It clattered up, easing itself awkwardly, a multi-purpose thing, a bright-orange, robotic farm-monster, almost exponential. It paused and snarled and thought for a moment about taking the little car up in its teeth and tossing it over into the apple trees. Sister Alfege turned her head as far away from it as possible and found herself looking down and sideways, through the spaces along the foot of the hedge, at a young leopard. It was lying in the celandines and lush new grass, frozen in the act of devouring something. It held the thing down – some rabbit, some rat – flapping open at the gut. With huge paws it dragged the bloody tendons upwards, head strained back. Its chops, fluffy and white, were spattered with blood. Its eyes, lamplit, crazy, became fixed on the face of the nun. It held its gaze steady. Then the car moved on.

'Are you all right, dear?' Sister Luke tried to get some sort of bearing on Sister Alfege in the driving mirror but could see only the metal rim of the wheelchair and the small black dome. 'Is all well?' Sister Reparatrice twisted round to try and see and said, 'She's sleeping. She's comfortable. She's in no pain.' Both Sisters thought of the ulcers on Sister Alfege's legs.

'She never took exercise. She never kept going,' said Sister Reparatrice, soon. 'No circulation. She was always feeble in the gardening.'

For some months Sister Alfege's legs had been too severe a case for the convent and the doctors at Ash had said that she now needed professional nursing. The Holy Rood would be the place and very shortly there would be a vacancy. Now the vacancy had come. A death – a phone call – and Sister Alfege was on the road with Sister Luke, who had taken other nuns on this journey and knew the ropes. Nobody had ever driven an empty car there to bring someone back.

'Isn't it the grand chair?' asked Sister Luke. 'Grand in scale to the car.'

'Will we be fetching it home with us?'

'That we shall not. We have to leave it. She'll maybe yet be able to sit out. It's not needed with us at present.'

'We can send for it after,' said Sister Reparatrice. 'Here's the zoo.'

They were winding down the last part of Bekesbourne Lane, on the old field path that has become a busy metalled road with motor coaches bringing animal-gazers for outings. A coach was approaching now with another behind it, both full of schoolchildren clutching wildlife trophies. They all looked beadily down at the carload of nuns as Sister Luke swerved again into the side of the road. 'They don't look excited at all,' she said, 'Not at all.'

'Children don't get excited any more.'

'Now how would we know, Sister Reparatrice? We see few enough.'

'The ones we see – with their parents in the shop and in the chapel—'

'And whatever's nuns and ruins to children?'

'Well, I'd have been wild for a zoo,' said Sister Reparatrice. 'Wild.'

'Now, there I'm with you. There I do agree. Is she all right, do you know? Can you see? Shall I draw up now and see to her?' They were near the motorway.

'She's grand. I'd find her her handkerchief but we're nearly there. I think she's sleeping. Oh, the legs!'

'The legs. It's terrible. See – here's the zoo entrance. It's the zoo where the keepers were killed, is it not? That was a terrible thing. Leopards, was it? I hear there's a memorial pillar. Now, that is nice.'

'It was tigers.'

'Tigers, was it? Well, I'd not choose to live too near. Not too near a zoo. There's no great fortifications. I'd not be surprised if they sometimes got out.'

'D'you know,' said Sister Reparatrice, 'as we stopped for that machine back at Littlebourne I thought I saw something in the hedge.'

'Something?'

'After the style of a leopard or a panther.'

'In the hedge?'

'Well, I dare say I had the zoo already in my mind.'

'I dare say you had. It would be a big tom cat now, Sister Reparatrice, or a fox.'

'I dare say so. A fox. The legs are terrible.'

'So they are. Put your handkerchief to your face, Sister Reparatrice.'

When they had deposited Sister Alfege at the Hospice, the two nuns walked back to the car and stood for a moment beside it, talking to the Mother Superior in the sunshine. She said, 'The poor soul. And isn't she over ninety? And wasn't she a German – one of the last ones?'

'Yes, though she speaks perfect English – that's to say, when she speaks at all, which isn't often now,' said Sister Luke.

'She's been in the convent here most of her life. She's nearly all in the spirit now, Reverend Mother.'

'Is it so? Now that surprises me.'

For Sister Alfege had been feverishly awake when they had taken her from the car, raising up her pink face to the blowy sky, nodding and smiling at the young nun who had put her in to bed and asking how soon she might get up from it again.

'Now I'm hoping to be up and about,' she had said.

'Well sure and you shall. You can go dancing on the roof, dear.'

'I'd like to sit in the window this afternoon and see the blossoms. Watch the spring coming.'

'And you shall, so.' (The window looked at the cement works.)

'And watch the cows, if possible, walking in the lane.'

'Cows it is.'

'At milking time.'

'All day long, dear.'

'And all the wild animals, too. First I'd like to watch the big cats. The panthers and the tigers, the leopards and the lynxes.'

'Every man jack of them. Give me your teeth, dear, for the glass. It's prayers in ten minutes. I think' – the nurse was turning away her face – 'we might find you the eau de Cologne before we do the dressings.'

★

'Terrible, the legs,' said the Mother Superior.

'It is herself rotting,' said Sister Reparatrice, who seldom dodged issues.

'Oh, we shall manage. We have met it before, and it will not be long, God willing. The ramblings—'

'About wild animals and such things, this last bit of the trip,' said Sister Luke. 'And she's never mentioned a breath of them before.'

'Dreams, no doubt. They have appeared to her in dreams. They'll be apocalyptic.'

'Maybe symbols from St Francis himself,' Sister Luke said. 'God rest her.'

'God rest her indeed,' said the Mother Superior waving them off, the bell behind her beginning to clang for compline. In her bed Sister Alfege was telling the suffering nurses of a wonderful soup served in her village at christenings made from the water that gushed from a stuck pig, and very rich.

'Strange, the leopard business,' said Sister Luke on the road. 'Could she have been aware of the zoo in some way? Would she have been listening? She'd never have known a zoo in her life.'

'No more do we.'

'Well, maybe it's no loss at that. I dare say we'd find them cruel places. Those beautiful creatures shut away for all their lives.'

'To be sure, but do you remember the hurricane? Quite a few creatures were said to get out in the hurricane and run about the fields all night and in the morning they were all queuing up at the gates to get in again. It was in the papers, I heard.'

'You will believe anything, Sister Reparatrice.'

'Well, and why not? Sister, this car. It still smells. I can scarcely—'

'We'll stop and open it up a bit. We might take a walk. We're in good time. There's little hurry. I'd have expected to stay longer.'

'She didn't seem to care whether we stayed or we didn't.'

'That's so.'

'Calling on about wild creatures all the time. We might never have brought her. We might never have been known to her. Not a word of a blessing.'

'Ah, she's away. She's far gone. She's nearly a hundred years old.'

Sister Reparatrice began to remember, and it became easier as they opened the two hatchback doors of the car and the sweet stench of decay floated out, that she had never liked Sister Alfege, even healthy. 'Leave them open as we walk,' she said.

'No, we'll just stand away a little bit. It's an invitation, leaving them wide. Windows maybe, but not the doors.'

'Who's to steal this old thing?'

'You never know. Give it a few minutes.'

They gave it a few minutes as they stood looking about them. They had stopped at a pretty place with a stile in a wooden fence and a wandering field path leading up a slope. 'I believe there's a church up there. Famously placed. Photographers go there and folk of that sort. Should we go up there ourselves now, Sister Luke?'

They shut the car doors but left the windows wound right down to show no glass and so appear to be shut. They crossed the stile and soon on the knoll became surrounded by little fruit trees that would next week be a sight for angels. The trees were not six-feet high, with chunky, ancient trunks, expertly pruned into springing new boughs above, studded with polished tight nuts about to explode into pink and white petals. The nuns touched them. 'They'll be older than the church,' said Sister Reparatrice. 'D'you see it? It's not old at all.'

'I'd say it might be. Look at the little faces on the porch all weathered nearly out. They're not human faces, whatever they are.'

'They'll be gargoyles.'

'This one has a snout. And a beard. And – well, it looks like a mane.'

Behind the church the fruit trees stopped to make way for tombstones and beyond them shaggy, moth-eaten larches towered, all shadows.

'I don't greatly care for this place,' said Sister Luke. 'It feels very cold. I think we're being watched. Maybe we should go in the church.'

So they turned back and passed between the little sandstone heads and tried the church door but it was locked. 'Nobody been here for years, I expect,' said Sister Reparatrice. 'Not a soul.'

'But one coming now,' said Sister Luke, as a man came out of the trees, carrying a gun.

He walked towards them and stood just outside the church porch, looking in. He was a red-haired, ferrety man in braces.

'Good afternoon,' said Sister Luke.

He looked at them – their black robes, their funny feet sticking out below.

'Animal out.'

'I beg your pardon?'

'Animal. Serval cat. From the zoo up Bekesbourne. Watch your two selves.'

'An animal *out*? Escaped?'

'You've not seen anything?'

Sister Reparatrice thought of the rustle and shimmer beyond the hedge. 'I saw something like a fox. Or a large cat. Oh, but it would be hours since.'

'Where?'

'Oh, near the zoo. As we were passing.'

'Going over into the farmer's field? By the orchards?'

'Well, I don't know. I dare say. We're from a distance. Yes, it was at the edge of an orchard.'

'We've seen it since then. We've hit it since then,' he said.

'*Hit* it?'

'Stunned it. With a dart. Anaesthetic. It ran for it. They can run a distance before they crawl off somewhere. It does them no harm but we want it back home before it comes round. Don't want it waking up again. Claw you alive. Keep your eyes awake, girls.'

'We're just leaving. We are going back to the car.'

'Keep your eyes open.'

In the Morris their excitement soon began to die and they fell silent. The same road. The same traffic. Doggedly Sister Luke put her foot down as they swung on to the mile and a half of motorway. Container lorries with foreign languages all over them from the Channel ports howled and shrieked their horns. The nuns looked anxiously for the sign to draw off the road on to the country lanes near the zoo again. They looked out for the cathedral across the meadows for a blessing, but missed it because of the gasworks in between. The sky clouded. Rain began and the day fell wretched.

Sister Luke began to say prayers to herself to mask her disappointment. It was more than a year since she had been further than two miles from the convent and she had set great store ('God forgive me! The poor soul') by the coming outing to take Sister Alfege towards her death. Sister Reparatrice sat rock-like beside her. 'Sure and we're spoiled,' thought Sister Luke. 'We're spoiled rotten, as the children say. Death is nothing. Death is only the passing through a negligible door. Death we welcome. Death is the opportunity for further service. Future glory.'

Yet up by that nasty church among those fruit trees, then away and down again by the blood-red dogwood of the hedges, the pumping of the sap, the tight calyxes of the apple blossom, the frilly cool petals of the primroses in the grass – such a surge of heart-breaking memory. Such an ache for some old earthly pain.

Hard-line Reparatrice had her handkerchief against her face again.

'Come now,' said Sister Luke. 'Don't keep at it, dear. The smell's gone.'

'It stays in the nose.'

'Never. Not on a day like this – look out at the spring.'

Sister Reparatrice watched the windscreen wipers.

'It's worse,' she said. 'It's stronger.'

'I've never had your nose,' said Sister Luke.

'Then you're very fortunate. This is a stench. That's what it is now – a stench. Bitter.'

'Well, she's gone. There's not even her chair or her rug. She's been gone an hour – maybe two. Maybe three – how long were we at that church? What is the time, I wonder? They have clocks in modern cars. It could be all of two hours.'

'I don't care,' said Sister Reparatrice; 'if you don't stop I'm going to vomit. I must get some air.'

'Very well, dear, if you have to.' She put on the footbrake, went into neutral, turned off the engine and took into her hand instead of the handbrake a long sinewy paw that lay flopped between the front seats.

'Oh, Christ, come quickly,' cried Sister Luke.

Both nuns fell out of the car from their respective doors and stood regarding one another on the most dangerous country roundabout in Kent. Rain fell on them and on all the coming blossoms.

'Look in,' said Sister Reparatrice in time. 'I am not able.'

Some motorbikes went roaring by, nearly hitting them. The angry screams of their horns faded into the distance.

'Look in.'

Sister Luke bent to look through the open back window. 'We must wind up the windows,' she said.

'Does it stir?'

'I think it's dead.'

The serval cat looked small lying limply on its back. Not very beautiful, like a wet fur coat chucked out for the rubbish. Its long narrow chest and stomach had softer hairs than the rough pelt on the legs. Its jaw was a chinless flat triangle, an upside-down slit with one long tooth looking out, dark yellow. The insides of the triangular ears were endearingly full of swan's-down and the long eyelids were sweetly closed.

'We stop the next car,' said Sister Reparatrice.

'There have been no cars. The zoo – the police may have closed the road.'

'There were the motorbikes.'

'They were maybe the last things through.'

'I think it stirred. Oh, Lord God – it did.'

'It did not. Not a whisker. Oh, look at them – look at the quills!'

'Quills? Oh, Mary, mother of God – has it quills?'

'The whiskers. Like quills. Wonderful,' said Sister Luke.

'That's blood on it. Blood on the chin and the chest. And the feet.'

Sister Luke looked down at her hand which had so lately clasped the creature's heavy paw, but it had left no blood.

'We'll start for the zoo,' said Sister Reparatrice. 'It's not a mile. It's not half a mile. We'll walk. Leave the car and walk.'

'No, no,' said Luke, 'we'll drive it there. There's nothing to fear. It's far away. Far away. It's dreaming of the jungle.'

'How do you know? How do you know what the

mind does in sleep? It could waken itself with its dreams. It could tear us to shreds. We'd be bravados to drive it.'

'Yet I've the feeling to drive it,' said Sister Luke, getting in behind the wheel again. 'Follow on your feet or get in.'

'I'll follow on my feet.'

Sister Luke, windows wide open, drove away.

'Stop!' cried out Sister Reparatrice. She scuttled up alongside, slid in like a frozen tree and got busy on her rosary. In ten minutes they were through the first gate of the zoo, which had near it a board on a post that said 'Animal Supplies Only'. They made for the main entrance of the zoo-owner's mansion and stopped the car at the foot of his Greek portico and wide flight of steps. Sister Reparatrice was out of the car, up the steps and at the bell.

Sister Luke got quite slowly out, however, looking down. She leaned in through the window and moved the errant paw into a more comfortable position. Then touched it again. Then she stroked a furry cheek. She did not touch the quills in case of activating some electricity. The animal looked peaceful. She surprised herself by thinking, 'If only poor Alfege had seen it.'

The adventure changed the two nuns. They did not go that way again. When Alfege died they stayed at the convent, allowing the other five to attend the funeral. Their separate memories somewhat changed the story as the years passed, and though it had quickly turned into famous folk-law in all the country round about they themselves steered clear of talking of it.

Once, years later, when Sister Luke had annoyed her

about something, Sister Reparatrice blazed, 'You have no sense of smell. It deprives you.' And once, scrattling up turnips in the sleet of an icy January, she said, 'You're slow and unhandy, Sister Luke.' And Sister Luke – so cold, so unlike her – spat back, 'It was I ran my hands down the pelt of it. It was I stroked its very cheek.'

THE MEETING HOUSE

There should be nowhere less haunted than the Quaker meeting house on High Greenside above Calthorpedale in the Northwest.

To get there it is best to leave the car on the byroad and walk up through the fields, for there are six gates to open and shut before you reach the deserted village of Calthorpe, which stands on a round lake that is shallow and silver and clean and still. The hamlet's short street and its empty windows and door frames are nearly blocked with nettles, its roofs long gone missing. A century ago, poor farming people brought up broods of children here on tatie pies and rabbits and broth and, very occasionally, some pork. The pigsty – one lank pig to a village – lies above the ruined houses. Behind the pigsty you take a track up the fell until you hit a broad grass walk nibbled to a carpet by sheep since James I's time and before. You come to two stone buildings to the right of the walk in the tussocky grasses. They are attached, one house bigger than the other.

When you get near you see that the smaller building is empty. A dark doorway gapes. There is not much roof left. But the creamy stone is bleached and washed clean by the weather and there are wild flowers and grasses round its feet.

The bigger building is one tall room within and is almost the oldest Quaker meeting house in England. George Fox himself is said to have preached here shortly after his vision of angels settling like flocks of birds on Pendle Hill. Its floor is the blue-white flagstones of the dale and there are three tiers of plain, dustless benches. The walls are dazzling white limewash and on a high stone shelf is a small paraffin stove and two now long-unused candlesticks. The Friends bring a medicine bottle of paraffin up the fell for making tea after worship but they don't bring candles, for the meeting house is used only on summer mornings now. It is a secure little place and bare. If walkers look through the clear glass in the windows they see nothing to steal.

The view from it is wonderfully beautiful and, as the Friends sit looking out through the windows and the open door across the dale to the purple mountains, a grassy breeze blows in; if Quakers believed in holy places this would be one of them. They do believe, however, in a duty to be responsible about property and thus it seems odd that the building alongside the meeting house should be derelict. But it had never been the corporate property of the Friends, being part of the estate of a local farming family who had been Friends for many generations and had used the little house as a lambing shed and springtime home of a shepherd who had doubled as the meeting house caretaker.

Those days are done. The farm has passed now to a consortium at York, the sheep are brought down to low pastures and shepherds today have motorbuggies and houses below the snow line. The meeting house caretaker was now Charlie Bainbridge, who had walked up to High Greenside once a week for years, at all seasons, and he had seen the smaller building left to fall gently down. Bainbridge, a huge old man, white-bearded and white-haired, was a still fellow who walked very upright without a stick even with snow on the ground. He said the long pull up to the meeting house was what had kept him healthy.

Hawks on the ridge had watched Bainbridge for years as he moved on a weekday morning across the valley floor, passing through the six field gates, fastening each one after himself, passing through the nettle-stuffed village, passing the muck-hard pigsty and away up beyond it to the broad grass track. On the common garth wall before the two buildings he sat down each week and ate his dinner out of a paper parcel and watched the weather coming and going. Larks and lambs in season, curlews at every season. Far too many rabbits. Disgraceful multitudes, he thought, remembering hard times and good stews of old. In winter there was often a stoat turned white, a rusty fox dipping a paw in snow. In April there were rainbows, often far below him and sometimes upside down. In May, a madness of cuckoos. A preserved and empty country.

He would consider the rain as it approached, watch the storms gather, the searchlights of sun piercing purple clouds and turning the fields to strobe-light, elf-light emerald. He sat waiting for the rain to reach him and wet him, the wind to knock him about. Until it did, he sat untroubled, like a beast. Then he got up and opened the meeting house door with the seven-inch iron key that lived under a stone, and plodded about inside maybe sweeping around a bit with the broom that lay under the benches. He looked out for cobwebs, trapped butterflies, signs of damp. Accumulated silence breathed from the building, wafted out on to the fell, swam in again like tides. Silence was at the root of Charlie's life.

So that when he was walking up one day and heard canned music he was jolted. He thought it could only be picnickers or bike boys cavorting about from over the west. They'd been seen about sometimes before. But then he saw that there were two big piles of rubble in front of the smaller building and clouds of lime dust floating in its dark doorway. Banging and crashing began to drown the music and then a dirty man came through the doorway carrying more rubbish and slung it on the tip. A child appeared, and then a very thin young grubby woman. The child was whining and the man aimed a kick at it. The woman swore at the man and the man said, 'Sod you. Shit.' The woman said, 'Leave it, will yer?'

Then the three stood looking at Bainbridge.

'Good day,' he said.

They said nothing. The man lit a cigarette.

'Can I help you?'

'Ye canna. We's 'ere. We's stoppin'.'

'Are you to do with them at York, then? The farming company?'

'We's 'omeless,' said the man. 'We's Tyneside.'

'See?' said the woman, and the baby stepped out of its plastic pants and defecated beside the rubbish.

'I come here,' said Bainbridge (in time), 'to see to the

meeting house. We don't use it often but it's our property. We are Quakers. The Society of Friends.'

'No friends of us,' said the man. 'Ye'll not shift us. You can't force us.'

'We wouldn't force you,' said Bainbridge, 'it's not what we do. We don't have violence. But we have a right of way into the meeting house across the garth.'

'Not now you haven't,' said the man, setting light to the rubbish.

Bainbridge left. He had never been a talker. Once or twice he had come across such people as these and had tried to understand them. Sometimes he had watched things about homelessness on somebody's television set and had always given generously to appeals for them that dropped through his door. But confronting them had been shocking, as shocking as meeting fallen angels, bewildering, frightening, disgusting and against natural order. When the Elders of the Meeting went up to High Greenside a few days later to investigate, Bainbridge stayed at home and planted onions.

The squatters at once made their position quite clear: they were not going, a point they made clearer still to the owner of the building who came over before long in a Merc from Harrogate. The owner, however, was not deeply worried. When he found that the family was not an advance party of vagrants or new-age travellers or a pop-music festival that might take root over his fields and settle there like George Fox's angels – fornicating, druggy, aggressive angels ruining pasture and stock – he said that at least the place was being used. The glass front door off a skip, the new metal windows set loose in the walls, the plastic chimneypot painted yellow and crazy tarpaulin slopped across the roof were matters for the National Park, not him. Carrying off an eighteenth-century rocking chair that the family had found in the rafters and also painted yellow, the owner said that he would of course have to tell the police.

'You do that.'

'I will. Oh, yes. Don't worry. I will,' he called and a Doberman who had been drooling and lolling with the baby in a broken chicken-wire playpen leapt at him with slippery turned-back lips, and man and chair fled down to the dead village.

'I'll give yer summat in rent when I'se in work, see? The wife's bad, see? She's had a tumour,' the man shouted after him. 'She likes it 'ere, see? Right?'

Next, a number of the Friends went up to explain to the family about the Sunday meetings and how, each week, they kept an hour of total silence at High Greenside. The music behind the glass door screamed and blared, the baby cried and it took a long time for the woman to answer their knocking. It was noon but she was in her nightdress.

'We sit in silence once a week. From ten-thirty until eleven-thirty on Sunday mornings. Only on six Sunday mornings. Only in summer. You are very welcome to join us.'

She said, 'Oh, yes. Yer comin' in?'

The flagstoned floor was still covered with lime dust and the sheep droppings of years had been heaped up with torn plastic bags of possessions – cracked shoes, rags, bottles, jars. There was a mattress with greasy coats across it and a new-looking television set and video recorder standing bewildered by the absence of electric sockets. In a little black hearth a fire of wormy sawn-up floorboards from the room above was burning, but the place was cold. The woman coughed, and behind the door that hid the stairs the Doberman boomed and clawed.

'You can't be very comfortable here.'

'It's OK.'

'We could help you. We have brought you a few groceries. And some runner beans and a stew.'

''E'd never.'

'Well, tell him we called. And about the silence on the Sundays.'

She wrapped a terrible matted cardigan more tightly around her bones. ''E'd never listen. 'E's that wild. One thing one minute, another the next.'

When they arrived the following Sunday the Friends found parts of old scrap-yard cars dragged across the garth and barbed wire fastened across their door. After negotiating all this and opening up the meeting house, they conferred, standing close together and thoughtful. The dog slavered and scraped inside the lambing-shed windows.

But seated soon on the familiar benches, their door open to a paradise morning, the dog quietened and the silence began. A different, answering silence from the house next door became almost distracting.

Or perhaps insolent; for the following Sunday the entry to the meeting house was blocked more thoroughly, this time with old roof beams, and, after they had struggled through these and silent worship had started, two transistors on different wavelengths were set outside on the party wall. An ill-tempered political argument fought with a programme of musical requests, both at full strength.

The next week it was a petrol-engine chain saw and for an hour its lilting scream, like cats in acid, seared the brain and ears and soul and a young Quaker who was a summer visitor from Leeds ran off down the hillside.

The noise was switched off the minute the hour ended and the clerk of the meeting, speaking slowly, said to the man lounging outside, 'By law, you know, you are meant to wear earmuffs when you're working one of these.'

The next week the man did wear earmuffs but the Quakers sat again in pain.

'What have you against us?' they asked as they locked up – now taking the key with them. Even Bainbridge looked shaken and drained. But the man said nothing.

The next week the saw broke down. The scream jolted and faded and died. It was a few minutes into the meeting and the man outside began to swear. He kicked and shouted, shouted and kicked, then stormed down to below the pigsty and shouted and kicked the tincan of his old pick-up van into action. Soon it could be heard exploding its way down through the fields.

The two transistors kept going when the sound of the pick-up had faded but their clack now was like balm and blessing after the saw; and a greater blessing followed, for soon they were switched off. The depth of the Quaker silence then was like hanging in clear water.

After a time, the child appeared in the open doorway quite naked – a queer, grey, dirty, sickly thing standing in the bright air. He tottered forward and flopped down and old Bessie Calvert, a gaunt stick herself, took him up on her lap, where he seemed to have no energy to do more than fall asleep.

When, in a few minutes, his mother stood in the doorway looking for him, Bessie moved a little and touched the seat beside her and the woman, again in her nightdress, threw her cigarette in the grass and came in. She sat sideways, twisted away from people, staring sulkily out of the door, but she sat, and when the car was heard returning she did not stir. And when the man and dog stood in the doorway she did not look at them. The dog's great chain was twice round the man's wrist and the chain rattled heavily as the dog dropped down to the ground, its chin on its paws. The dog sighed.

Then the man pulled the dog away and they both stood outside in the garth, the man leaning against the meeting house wall. 'Good day,' said the Quakers passing him by at the end of the hour (there had been no tea-making this summer), holding out their hands as usual, one after another. As usual the hands were ignored but leaning against the wall the man gazed far away and said nothing. He looked very tired.

As they went off down his voice came bawling after them.

' —Next week, mind. Not an end of it. See what we do next week. Settle your silences. You'll not get rid of us. You's'll never be rid of us. We's after your place next.'

But the next week nobody was there. All were gone,

the family, dog, car, television set, chain saw, the few
poor sticks of furniture, the new padlock for the pathetic
glass door that now stood open on the foul mattress, piles
of nappy bags, flies and a mountain of sawn wood. A
jam jar of harebells stood on a stone sill with a note under
it saying, 'Sorry we had to go. We'd got started liking it
up here.' In the paper the following Wednesday the
Friends read that at about the time they had been reading
the note the whole family and its dog had been killed in
their wretched car on the M6 just below Tebay.

Quakers accept. Grief must be contained, translated.
Friends do not as a rule extend themselves over funerals.
But three of the Quakers from High Greenside did attend
this one far away over in Cumbria and later on Charlie,
Bessie and the clerk cleaned out the old lambing shed,
removed the rubbish – the tarpaulin, the mattress – to the
tip twelve miles off. They distributed the firewood and
disposed of the sagging little chicken-wire playpen. They
worked thoroughly and quietly but found themselves
shaken beyond all expectation.

The playpen and the now withered harebells in the jar
brought them close to weeping.

It was during the following winter that stories began.
Walkers were puzzled by canned music that came from the
High Greenside buildings and faded as they drew near.
Fishermen down by the lake at night sometimes heard
the barking of a great dog. Across the dale, people saw a
light shining like a low star on the fell-side from where
the empty buildings stood. After Christmas the

Yorkshire farmer came back with his wife to inspect but
had to turn away because the wife for no reason suddenly
became very much afraid. Charlie Bainbridge was
thankful that the snow came early and deep that year and
stopped his weekly visit – not because of ghost talk, he
had no belief in ghosts, but because the place now
distressed him. When the snow melted he was in bed
with chronic bronchitis brought on by the long indoor
months. He grew better very slowly.

So that it was almost summer again before he got up to
the meeting house once more. Rather thinner but still
upright, he set off soon after his dinner one day in early
May. He walked steadily, opening and shutting each gate
as before, circling the silver shilling of the lake, through the
bad village, up beyond the pigsty to the wide grass ride. It
was a balmy, dreamy day. He was happy to be back. The
bank rising to the far side of him was rich with cowslips.
Rabbits as usual. A lark in a frenzy, so high he could
scarcely see it. As he came near the two pale buildings he
said, 'Well, now then Very good. Swallows is back.'

He stopped and for the first time in many months
looked down and across the sweep of the dale, the black
and silver chain mail of the walls, the flashing sunlight.
'Grand day,' he said aloud and turned to find the
Doberman standing before him across the path.

Then it was gone.

He looked over at the meeting house, but did not
move. He heard a thread of music, then silence. He
wondered if he heard laughter.

The silence grew around him again and he waited. He
tried out some remarks to himself.

'Here's some puzzle,' was the first.

'I stand here,' was the second.

'Let's see now what it's all about,' was the third.

He walked forward to the common garth, opened the gate and looked into the derelict building. Nothing. The grass was growing again in the flagstoned floor. He walked along to the meeting house and looked through the windows. Nothing. Not a shadow. The place seemed to have wintered well. A clear light flowed in over the bare benches. All quite empty.

But then he saw them, all three together, on one of the long seats. It was not a vision, not a moment of revelation. There seemed nothing ghostly in it. The man had an arm along the back of the settle and the night-dressed, bare-foot woman had the child on her knee and had folded herself in against the man's shoulder. They looked very familiar to Charlie Bainbridge, like old friends or, as it might have been, his children. And yet changed: confident, peaceful, luminous, beyond harm, they were all gazing outward from the meeting house, intent and blissful in the quiet afternoon.

THE DAMASCUS PLUM

....

The better the soil, they say, the uglier the country; but I have never found East Kent ugly. The miles of crumbly light-coloured silt that were once swum over by North Sea fishes look lovely at all times – blue with a million rows of cabbages in autumn, green and cream with big, hard, smelly cauliflowers, purple with radicchio in summer and here and there – and at last, for it has been gone since 1939 – water-blue with delicate flax. Inward from Deal and seaward from Canterbury is a vast market garden, and miles of kitchen garden flank the roads. Rough painted signs with unusual spellings are stuck up on boards saying 'Hay, walnuts, cobs' and below the boards on trestle tables there is sweet corn so cheap it is almost free. You gather up a basket of huge fat pods and put some bits of money in a tin.

Then in winter the thready black aisles of the hop garden wires and poles make cat's cradles round the coast, with white sky above. Lettuce leaves in late spring lie in acres along the edge of the golf course near the sea at Sandwich Bay, looking like petals resting before being blown away to Belgium. A week or so later, with the sprinklers flinging themselves about above them, they are all sitting up straight and nicely rooted. Sometimes you see lettuces lying about for the picking up, as you see cabbages growing naturally wild – their arrival related to the ancient Romans – along the White Cliffs of Dover. Stray cauliflowers after the harvest roll about at the field sides like severed heads after a revolution. Walking in the orchards near Paramour Farm last year I came on a six-foot-tall hill of dumped gooseberries, waxy and gold as crystallized fruit and fizzing with wasps. Under the little regimented fruit trees are apples the pickers have missed, bright trickles and pyramids of scarlet and crimson and green and yellow. On the top of each tree an apple or two left for luck. Sometimes a vast field of peas turned golden, left to rot. East Kent with a hard cold climate and hard-headed people can cope with abundance, even extravagance, when it comes to fruit and veg.

And with destruction. Apple orchards, so heart-breakingly lovely and looking fit for the next hundred years, disappear overnight; and then before you've quit mourning you see another great square of young ones planted out to replace them.

And in the shops in Sandwich and Deal and round Fordwich and Worth you don't go asking for apples but for Discoveries or Greensleaves or John o'Golds, and potatoes are never potatoes but almost always Desirées. A half-mile line of eighty-foot poplars on the skyline that you've believed an ancient landmark is suddenly not there, and nobody minds. It's back again three years later, sprouting up even stronger and already as high as a house. The tiny vineyards, five or six of them and none more than a few acres, are spruce as France and worked at with ferocious determination, and when any of them wins an international prize they fly a flag.

Everyone is serious about fish, too. In Deal there are five fish shops and two at least have their own boat. There are fishermen's genes in Deal. I once saw three small boys dragging something large and grey and uncommonly like a dead mermaid towards Griggs's in South Street – for an opinion only, I'd guess. I don't see such a thing being offered for sale.

There is no smell of fish in these fish shops, only of fresh salt water and the seaside, so that you don't even bother to telephone to see what's on sale if there's been a storm. Nothing, if the boat has stayed on the shingle. A little frozen fish is kept, but almost out of sight and not for the locals.

Most days, though, fresh fish is stacked on the marble slabs, and not arranged in scaly ceramics as in London, for there's no time for that. It sells too fast. You see people choosing things that are seldom seen in inland towns – huge parcels of bright silver sprats (for twenty pence a pound); large whiskery things in shells; and great big sunset-coloured undressed crabs. You see children on the shoulder being given a twist of paper full of prawns and not an ice cream or a Big Mac in sight; and there was an old girl in the other day wearing a balaclava and sawn-off gloves buying a big belligerent black lobster. 'It's for me friend. It's her birthday.' It scarcely sounds English. Is it French? Is it perhaps the inter-mingling of French blood from across the water? Just try suggesting it.

The social elite of this part of East Kent makes its way for fish to the tiny shop between Deal and Walmer facing the sea and owned by Messrs Cavell. Here you stand in reverent silence and politely away from the counter while a Mr Cavell whispers recommendations – and instructions about cooking, if you should ask – to his customers, one by one. There is never anything so plebeian as a queue at Cavells and there is very little fish to be seen, though the brothers C smoke their own cod and haddock and pot their own shrimps and you can negotiate for their hung game. At intervals both Mr Cavells – or are there three? – will disappear behind a screen to an inner sanctum, like Orthodox priests at the holy part of the service, and little clinking noises of ice and sharp knives and rushing water can be heard. The fish are brought for silent inspection, then operated upon behind the screen, brought back for re-inspection, emerging at last, wrapped in quantities of fresh grease-proof paper, to be exchanged for a large amount of money. To be invited out to dinner by someone who can cook and lives in reach of any of these East Kent fish shops is an invitation I'd prefer to one at almost any restaurant, in almost any country. Yet do they know this in the rest of Europe? No, they do not, which shall be exemplified in the story of my one-time pupil, Klaus the Swiss, whom I met many years ago in East Kent and then again this summer, in his full majesty, on the shores of Lac Léman near the discriminating city of veal and cream, Geneva.

I had been told of the boy Klaus by a woman I hardly knew who was a friend of Klaus's English uncle and two aunts who lived together in a village nearby to Eythorne. They had just adopted Klaus. His mother, the third of the sisters, had died earlier in the year. She had married a Swiss who had died some years before and the uncle and aunts were trying to get the boy into an English public school for which he had to pass the Common Entrance examination.

'*Very* clever,' the woman told me. '*Very* bright. English perfect but – well, I expect they'll explain. Though they're not talkative themselves. They're naval.'

'Navel?' I thought of oranges. Of birth.

'The brother was R.N. and one of the sisters was a Wren. Mad on the land like retired naval people get. None of them ever married. You know the picture. It's getting rare that sort of set-up. There's a difficulty with the imagination somewhere. They're a bit silent. You do this sort of coaching, don't you? Yes, I thought you did. They'd be ever so grateful.'

The house where this family lived turned out to be over the flat field-side lanes inland from the sea, a mile or so through Sholden and beyond haunted Northbourne, then through the cornfields on the narrow lanes. It was a lovely, still September afternoon and I pedalled along following the signposts, passing one deserted grassy crossroads after another and the odd white windmill against the sky. Klaus's village was up a narrow road marked as a dead end which stopped being metalled as it became the village street. The house – it was called Plum Cottage – was at the far end of this and looked out on both sides and from the back at fields, a river, sleeping elms and beeches. Fat black cows strolled along the river bank. The sky was huge. The small straggled village seemed deserted and asleep.

The boy himself came to the door and stood holding the

latch. It was mock medieval and there was a mock-medieval lantern attached to the wall nearby and below it a board saying 'Plum Cottage' in pokerwork. As the boy stood back for me to pass I could see through the cottage, where there seemed to be little furniture but a great many wellington boots, to the garden where a stalwart but shadowy person was working in a rose bed. Over the cottage door late roses were splayed on do-it-yourself-shop fans of neat plywood. They had metal tags on them. The tall boy, holding the latch, between the roses, stood spotty, rebellious, leathern-lidded, sullen-eyed, limp-handed and so sadly thin he seemed concave. I thought he looked at me with distaste but then thought perhaps it was misery.

Round the corner of the front of the house came one of the aunts, presumably the ex-Wren, trundling a great wheelbarrow and we turned back to her as she set it down on the path. As we talked, she took a piece of bread roll out of her pocket and began to eat it. Then, as the boy and I went into the house and down the passage towards the study at the back, a second aunt peeped out of the kitchen, which seemed to be full of trays of cuttings in plastic pots. On the table was a family-sized tin of soup, two small tins of baked beans and a packet of sliced white bread. As the boy and I sat down at the uncle's desk facing the window the shadowy man in the garden stepped out of the flower bed and passed us by, making a sketchy naval salute but not looking at us. Later I noticed him standing by the compost heap peeling a banana. He dropped the peel meticulously on the heap and then, after a moment, threw the banana in after it.

★

Klaus was clever all right, whatever clever means. He was an astonishing linguist, his English not only utterly confident but idiomatic, colloquial and quite accentless. He said that his French and German were about equal to his English and his Spanish was 'coming on'. Mathematical subjects, he said, had 'never been any trouble' to him and I believed it, for I soon found that he had a piercing rational faculty.

But I was here to teach him how to write the compulsory imaginative essay for the examination and of doing this he had no notion at all. We went through several specimen papers but every title I suggested he might try he treated with a small derisive smile. 'It cannot be done,' he said. 'This one – "Travelling". It isn't possible. It's not precise.'

'Then say so. Discuss it.'

'That wouldn't be very polite, would it? Impolitic too. It would antagonise them.'

'Not at all. Or not necessarily. Klaus, you're being too literal. Too serious. Just get down *something*. You know about travelling.'

'I've only travelled once. By air from Geneva to Gatwick airport, and by car to this house.'

'Well, that's more than a lot of people have done. You can talk of travelling even if it's just over the fields. Over there. From this room. Just walk through the garden down to the river. That's travelling. Watching the cows is travelling. Sitting still and thinking can be travelling. Think of the – concept.'

'Who would want to know about all that?'

'Well – you have to make it interesting, so that they will.'

'But it doesn't make me interested.'

'Well, then—'

Another lesson later in the week. '—Well, then, what does interest you? Let's work from the other way round.'

'Maths does. And translating. And—' His blank eyes swivelled away from me and he stared out at the evening light. His uncle was not on the scene tonight but a wicker chair with a pale squashy cushion stood under the three little trees beside the wall of old bricks called soft Kent reds. The uncle's hat lay on the grass and the colour in the flower beds was glowing and saddish as the day began to fade. I remembered that Klaus had lately lost his mother and had had no father for years.

'Do what you can with it,' I said. I saw to it that he had all the notes I had written for him, suggestions for various treatments of various subjects and some other essays he could consult. He walked me as usual most politely to the door and past the kitchen where the second and more female and landward of the aunts stood at an old gas stove burning a pan of baked beans. 'Oh dear,' she called, 'I'm afraid we're not great cooks here. The garden is too big for us.'

I caught Klaus's eye and felt for the first time his huge remoteness from the house. He was far out of his depth here, scarcely swimming. Over the next weeks, as Klaus and I sat in tortured struggle to unlock one shred of his soul, the smell of burning food and the haphazard munching of his ambulant relations began to attack my nervous system, too.

Once, as I heard his stomach give tongue I brought out

some chocolate from my bag and broke it up and laid it on the desk. He pushed it about.

'Go on. Eat it.'

'I only eat Swiss chocolate, thank you.'

'Try this.'

'No. What I want is just a meal. Just to sit down to a meal.'

'All right,' I said, 'I'll get you some Swiss chocolate next time. Look, describe to me. Describe to me what *hunger* is. What hunger feels like.'

He looked amazed once again. 'There's nothing to say. It – well, it is unpleasant of course.'

'Like? Well, think of something that it is like.'

'This is what you've been saying – a metaphor?'

'Exactly. Use one. Make one.'

'It feels— It is like itself. Hunger. There is no comparable situation, I feel.'

'Oh, for God's sake! Look [I would be rash. I would be cruel] – just describe something else, then – something that's unpleasant. Describe death. Tell me about it.'

'How can I? I have not died.'

'Very well, then. Your mother is dead. Describe to me your mother's death. Tell me about it. Go on.'

'I was not present.'

'Well, describe how you were told of it. How – were you in the house at the time? In the hospital?'

'It was a clinic.'

'Describe the clinic. What happened. *Now* – get on. I'll go out of the room if you like.'

'That's all right.'

I went out to the garden and walked over to the three damson trees. Their trunks were covered in silver, white-green fluffy bark and they felt warm. The little blue-black fruits clustered in the flutters of pale leaves and silver branches. A small heap of black, spiky sawn branches lay in the grass where the uncle had been gathering them up for firewood. Some were heavy, dense, silver, leaden wood, old as the wall they had grown against and older, and in them the smell of last-century summers, all forgotten. Oh, how to reveal something, anything, of this to the boy.

He came dragging his big feet over the grass with his essay on death dangling from his hand. It read something like this:

> At 13.40 my mother was in a plastic hood of oxygen and held a machine in her hand. The hospital was very well organised and effective and when a nurse told me that through the plastic my mother would be unable to hear me speak and communication would thus be impossible I accepted what she said. She suggested that I might like to go for a cup of coffee in the office at the end of the ward. This I did and at 13.50 heard some people hurrying along the corridor outside and I saw a doctor go by. At 13.59 the nurse came to inform me that my mother was dead.

'Klaus. Well, Klaus. Do go back. In your head. *Remember.*'

He sat down in the creaking chair and stared up at the plum trees. He wrote on the pad:

> They asked me almost at once (14.20) if I would like to take home my mother's wedding ring as it would only be taken otherwise by the funeral furnishers and perhaps lost. At 14.30 they brought it and her other belongings. At 14.33 I declined to see the body of my mother, saying that I wished to remember her as in life. I had heard of

this being said. They offered me more coffee and asked if there was someone at home I might like to come to the hospital to take me back, but I said no to both suggestions and (14.40 approx) I left the hospital.

'Klaus—'

'Listen,' he said, 'Lizzie—' I had a flicker of hope. 'Lizzie, my mother wasn't a very nice woman. I didn't mind her dying.'

'I give up,' I said and we both stared at the trees. The little plums looked back at us. The silver bark shone pinkish for a moment in the evening sun.

'What sort of a plum is that?' asked Klaus.

'It's a damson. We love it in England. It's a very old plum. Part of our history. It's been here for hundreds of years. It's called "the Damascus plum". St Paul must have eaten it once, in Syria.'

'Does it taste good?'

'Very good when it's cooked. It's sharp. A very strong plum. It needs sugar. Wonderful with cream – the two colours together—'

'I've never tasted the Damascus plum.'

On the way home along the lanes, over the raised field paths, past the windmill standing in the flax, I thought, 'Poor little nothing. Poor little priggish, pompous nothing. What has someone done to you to bring you so low? Or could he possibly have been born like that?' 'He shall,' I said, 'he *shall* tast the Damascus plum.' And I rang up the austere aunts to invite Klaus to Sunday lunch with us. 'To *luncheon*,' I said (and think of that while you're weeding the lobelias).

'*Luncheon*. At 12.30.' They seemed both puzzled and

delighted. 'How very kind. We don't go in for –
luncheon – very much here, I'm afraid. Especially just
now, with all the fruit. Are you sure?'

'Spotted dick and custard, then?' asked my husband.
'Prepare him for an English school, poor boy. Ginger
pud? Kate and Sydney?'

'No. You'll see. Most certainly not.'

'And do we produce a glass of wine for this fourteen-
year-old or some cans of coke?'

'Somehow I'd think wine.'

'I'll buy it from the supermarket. I'm not getting
anything up for him.'

'What about us?'

'Well, all right. Maybe we'll need something good to
get us through. Why we have to do all this when you say
he's dreadful. A human being with nothing that interests
him at fourteen! My God!'

'There may be. Let's see.'

'What are we having?' asked my husband en route for the
cellar the evening before the luncheon. 'You mean we're
having fish *and* meat? For Sunday *lunch*?'

'And cheese. And pudding. Damson tart – open
damson tart. And I'm making tartlet things with pâté
for beforehand. Then the fish. Yes. Then roast beef and
Yorkshires, as he's never heard of them, and I'm doing a
mush of courgettes and broccoli with herbs and good
English mustard made with balsam vinegar, and gravy
made from pheasant stock and wine. And Bolivian
coffee. And then he's staying to tea.'

'Are you in love?'

'He is revolting. But I won't have him revolted. He's in England to learn. He shall learn that we can cook and I'm his teacher.'

We had Cavells' little lemon soles, hot and curly and light and crisp, in breadcrumbs and with lemon juice. Then we had sirloin of Scotch beef, not *en croûte* but just as juicy; and green vegetables and small carrots with parsley butter and chopped, uncooked onion. The potatoes (Desirées, of course) I parboiled and then shoved far back in the top of the oven for seventeen minutes in hot olive oil. 'Extra virgin olive oil,' I said, and when Klaus asked 'What is an *extra* virgin?' and my husband said, 'Maybe it's a nun,' Klaus actually laughed.

The extra virgins came out of the Aga like golden, crunchy, soft-centred flowers. Then we had redcurrant water ice, the redcurrants from Rusham Farm, and for the damson tart a jug of cream from Solley's Farm at Worth, thick and yellow. The cheeses were Cheddar – I'd spent a long time choosing the finest of five good ones – a local chèvre and a perfect double Gloucester.

The pastry for the tart was the best I had ever made. I'd iced the knife as well as the water and the bowl. It was crisp but flaky. Almost transparent. The damsons sat darkly inside it basking in a congealing sticky lake of crimson juice and sprinkled with hard brown sugar. They looked comfortable as fat black ladies in a spa.

On and on Klaus ate. And we ate. He sat pink and absorbed and silent. In a final dizzy flourish I spun out into the kitchen and in a minute or so came back with a pancake for him filled with maple syrup. It rustled as I slid it on to its hot plate.

We'd asked him if he'd like a glass of wine with the beef and slowly, seriously, he drank two. 'Chassagne-Montrachet,' he said to my husband. 'Thank you very much, sir.' He had a glass of English wine with the ice and pronounced it very good, 'very like a Riesling'.

My husband said, 'Well! If you were not fourteen years old I believe I'd offer you a Barsac with the plums,' and Klaus said, 'Thank you. I should like that very much. I don't think that my age is of any consequence. My father taught me to drink sensibly. He was a wine merchant.'

'But surely—' said I, 'hasn't your father been dead for some years?'

'Yes. I was nine. I suppose I'd better walk home. You mustn't drive me and I'll have to cool off before Plum Cottage.'

We walked first, though, along the sea-front a little, and looked across at the navy-blue line of France. It was very clear that afternoon. Rain was coming. I said that France seemed to be making a statement, some metaphor was there, but Klaus was not interested. He said soon, 'Did you mean it that I might stay on for tea? I've not had an English tea.'

'What was your English mother about?' we asked.

'Oh, she was another gardener,' said Klaus.

For tea – I had more than intended him to stay; I had exerted myself – we had small thick triangles of rye bread and butter, small thin triangles of white bread and butter, scones with butter and home-made strawberry jam in a glass dish with the strawberries hanging whole in the jelly, suspended like rubies. We had Sally Lunn and Sad Mary and sponge cake with jam in the middle and icing on top – plain white. We had fresh lemon-curd tarts and raspberry tarts, each the size of a fifty-pence piece and light as flakes. We had an English Swiss roll, not sticky and with bitter chocolate filling, not sickly black cherries. And – bother the boy, it had taken five hours – we had an old English Lenten Simnel cake soaking with soft marchpane, soft as honey, light as air.

And somehow we got him home to his aunts.

'You are of course mad,' said my husband, 'but at least there is now one Swiss in the world who won't forget that the English respect food. It's a blow struck for international understanding. Whether he'll pass the essay paper of course is another matter. My guess is no.'

But Klaus passed. There was a miraculous option in the essay paper, '*The Pleasures of the Table*', and as far as I could make out he wrote out lists of interesting menus and recipes and a short treatise on wine. The examiner must have been his fairy godfather – and he must also have been somewhat surprised. The aunts and uncle sent me a huge pot plant with my fees and Klaus wrote a very formal thank-you letter. He became a Swiss lawyer and we kept in touch for years until, as happens, it got down to Christmas cards only. The Christmas cards fizzled out, and we forgot him.

Then, last year on holiday in Geneva, we read in the newspapers that he had been appointed a Swiss cantonal judge, and the news was too tempting to ignore. We wrote our congratulations and the next day he was speaking to us on our hotel's telephone. And he invited us to dine.

Oh, such a benign and gigantic man came forward to greet us! Oh, the manner of Methuselah, tall as he was vast, pale, portentous and very slow! Most thoughtful of speech. His voice was tiny, like the voice of a bat; but perhaps that is so of all cantonal judges since they have to speak to an empty court room – which is the only eccentricity in Switzerland I ever heard of. Admittedly it's a big one.

He had brought his wife to meet us and they took us to dine at the best of all gilded and velvet Genevan restaurants, where the menu was like the Swiss themselves, short, rich and unadventurous. The wine was very like the white of St Nicholas at Ash, but when I said so Klaus only gave his small mysterious smile, to hide non-comprehension. Well, it was thirty years ago.

We thanked profusely, of course, and Klaus's round-faced cheery wife said what a pleasure it had been for them to entertain us. *And*, she said, how lovely it must be for us to be in Switzerland and get away from the English weather, and the food. 'Not that I've ever been there,' she said. 'It's only what one hears. It's probably folklore.' I told her that the English weather was wonderfully varied and not what she thought, and I waited for Klaus – I watched him and I waited – for a word about the food.

It was so very, very long ago, but surely, surely, some little memory might stir? The soles from Cavells, the Elysium Yorkshire puds, the tartlets, the pancake, the Sally Lunn, the superb cheese, the basking black ladies?

Surely some frail memory must be left in the mind of the doleful, rational gourmet, the so very hungry boy on his one, luscious English day.

'I have never been back,' he said. 'But I remember things about England.

'About Kent,' he said. 'There were some beautiful little plum trees. They were, I think, in your own garden, Lizzie? Oh, such a good-looking little dark plum and it ate beautifully. Not English though, I am afraid. I believe it came from somewhere in the Middle East.'

DEAD CHILDREN

The blackberry bushes were much as they had always been in October – silvery, black, purple and red, hanging in swags, dense in their hearts. Many berries were still to be gathered, many gone mouldy and dropped, or about to drop, in little chinchilla balls on the turf inside the glade. Since the days when she had walked there as a young woman with her children there had been dramatic happenings on the common: a raging fire, a blight of grasses, and incredibly, once, a hurricane that had tipped high trees about like chess-men. The trees had lain on their sides humiliated, huge discs of roots blatant to the sky.

But the bramble bushes had survived, always springing ing up again for new generations to wander in with plastic bags and purple hands. The children were differently shaped now, in unisex boiler suits and jeans and blocky canvas shoes. Her children had been in dresses and shorts, buckled sandals and white socks. Thirty-five years ago.

Though leaner, vaguely ancient and walking more slowly, Alison Avery felt much the same now as then: lighter and happier in some ways, for she was very free now. She didn't gather blackberries any more and there was no husband to go home for, but she felt, if anything, rather more her true self at eighty-two without these distractions.

Blackberries. Her flat got messy enough without blackberries. They were useless as presents. All her friends were her own sort of age now and avoided pips. Preserving pans had been handed over long ago to children or grandchildren, or good causes. One was given jam – or tactful jelly – now. Mrs Avery had always dreaded the time when she would be in receipt of little pots of jelly.

But she loved the glade, the springing curves of the branches, the dusty tunnels underneath. Lately, a seat had appeared in the midst of them on the handkerchief of green grass, placed there in memory of some dog who had 'roamed these commons for many years'. The seat had the dog's name and its dates inscribed on a plaque. The seat had been put there only this March and nobody else seemed to have found it.

In the days when Mrs Avery had brought her children here, they had all sat on the patch of secret grass and spread a cloth for picnics. Now she lowered herself slowly on to the slats of wood, sighing.

She was utterly separated from the world here. Wanderers, wankers, molesters, muggers and, once, a murderer had visited the common since the long-ago picnics. Not safe on the common any more they all told each other, and probably if anyone knew of her sitting here alone there would be a fuss. 'Aged Titania in her bower,' she thought.

It was particularly quiet today, the time between lunch and tea, before the schools were out and while the smallest children would still be resting. Nobody in the world knew where she was. She closed her eyes and listened to the silence.

'And after such a hateful lunch,' she thought, 'and such pain.'

The lunch had had to do with the future. Mrs Avery found nowadays that consideration of the future was a bad idea. Or of the past, come to that. And in spite of her increasing confusions she held firm to this belief. The drowsy autumn common, the fat and fecund, eternally recurring, eternally swelling, eternally dropping blackberries, the eternal voices of children passing along the hidden rides on the cinder track towards the windmill.

'It's mine!' 'No, it's *mine*.'

– so school must be out –

'Come here, you're filthy.'

'But look what I've *found*!'

'Quickly, we must—'

'Millions of blackberries. *Millions* of blackberries.'

'We must get back. I've lost the car keys. Where's the damn dog?'

All this she heard without listening, let it all pass over her. 'Let it wash,' she thought, 'over my uncertain head. My foolish, feeble head.'

The purpose of the lunch had been her will. Her children, Pete and Annie, had come from great distances and arrived efficiently together on her doorstep, at the time arranged, and arranged only after much discussion, for this had been the second or third attempt at meeting. They were all three to talk over luncheon about inheritances at the splendid new château of a hotel that now stood on the common and was reputed to be a place for a special occasion.

So they had walked there. Past the shallow pond, through the magnificent new gates to the hotel's glossy façade and found po-faced waiters standing about, fat quilted curtains all satin and swags and a very few people sitting at chilling distances from each other. Half of them were Japanese, frozen and bewildered by the silence and wishing they had stayed in central London.

The place had been an old-folks' home when Pete and Annie were children. Annie had once crawled up the bank from the park behind the mansion, under the chains on to the terrace (now decked out with white furniture and plastic plants) to press her face against the glass of the saloon and frighten such inmates as could still look towards the outside world.

'Why do they sit sleeping in a ring? One of them has a long bit of spit hanging.'

'They're just old,' Mrs Avery had said to her and Annie had looked intent. She had been five. Her round sun's face surrendered to another sun of flames of golden hair, silky and shiny. Her eyes turned up to her mother were unwary, wide, amazed. Mrs Avery knew that her daughter was encountering death.

'Will *I* get old?'

'Oh yes – but it will be all right.'

On the way home Annie had asked, 'Will you get old?'

'Not like that. I give you my promise. I have decided. Nor will you.'

'Or Daddy? Or Pete?'

'Certainly not.'

Annie had climbed into the buggy then and gone to sleep, slumped peacefully sideways. On the slow trail home with the disobedient, dawdling dog refusing to catch up and then entangling itself round wheels and legs, Pete had put his warm hand over hers on the buggy handle. He'd said, 'Oh, I expect we'll all get old!'

Remembering his calmness and wisdom at six, his grave, sweet face, Mrs Avery had marvelled this morning at his ferocity. Such a man would have terrified the long-ago small boy. She had marvelled although she had known now for years this snarling stranger.

The mansion-restaurant, cleansed now of its aged, and pulsating with rather precarious self-esteem, had refused Pete admittance because he was wearing jeans. And no tie.

'But this is after all a Saturday morning. And we have booked a table.'

'It is a rule, sir.' And not even Annie, head of a county council, her Jaeger suit and good pearls, her authority born of successful marriage, successful divorce, four impressive, successful children, had touched the *maître d'hôtel*, a trivial, icicle man, enclosed in his job.

So, feeling very overdressed, Alison Avery, Pete and Annie had gone back over the common to a pub and a table ringed with beer, where big T-shirted fledglings, all stubble and armholes, had shouted each other down against loud music, and empty glasses and paper cups lay about outside in the shabby grass. Pete and Annie fumed.

'I wouldn't live in this place now,' said Pete. 'God! –

bourgeois, vulgar, stinking rich, semi-educated – *foreign*.'

'And we moved here because it was so cheap,' said his mother, 'and so unspoilt. It was like the Edwardian countryside here when you were both born. I remember thinking, "I can bring them on the common every day. Every day of the week they can run in the grass—" After London it was – oh, so easygoing here, so peaceful.'

'Well, it's not peaceful now,' said Pete. 'We'll have to try and talk somewhere else. Back in the flat? Or maybe just leave it? Some other day?'

Annie said, 'Oh, no! Not after all this. I haven't another day. Not before Christmas.'

'But Christmas is three months away,' said her mother.

'That's the way it is. I work,' said Annie.

Pete, who lived a mysterious freelance life and was rich (the jeans were from Rome and bore a famous name), said that Annie had never learned to delegate.

'No. I have not. I'm glad to say. This is why I'm where I am.'

'Which is?'

'Oh, do stop!' Mrs Avery looked down at her brick of black lasagna.

'Look – we could go to the flat, but there is really no room for three to sit. We could talk on the common. Shall we just talk on the common? We could find a place to sit there.'

'No,' said Pete. 'No. I hate to say it but actually this is providential for me. I didn't tell you after the other fiascos, but I had to put something off to come here

88

today. In London. Quite big. I could still just get there. I'd rather leave this business for now if possible. I mean it. You're not going to die today, Ma. You look wonderful. We'll see you home. And we've *seen* you – we've had the lunch. That was part of it, wasn't it?' he added, placatory and brightish. Then ferociously he looked towards Annie, who was flicking intensely about in her diary. Mrs Avery set down her fork. 'D'you know, I think I'd *like* to call it off today,' she said. 'Later – this is what I'd really like – later I would like to come and see one of you at home, probably Annie, and Pete perhaps you could join us there? Stay overnight with us. I'd like to stay the night with you both, darling Annie. And we could take our time.'

'Or we could make a date with the solicitor and hire Mum a car and all go to Gray's Inn sometime,' said Pete.

'No. I won't do that,' said Annie.

'Why ever not?'

'It looks inhuman. Calculating. I hate talking about wills like that. Anyway, we've both got plenty.'

'Oh, but it would be worse if you hadn't,' said Mrs Avery, feeling rather tender. Annie glared at her.

'Come on, Ma,' she said, 'let's get you back to the flat, you'll be exhausted.'

'It is *not* inhuman to talk of wills,' said her mother, 'and I *want* to do some calculating. We have a good solicitor who knows about settlements. I like Smithson. I liked his father and I like him, and I need professional advice. But I want you with me. I know you're both clever enough – but I want no quarrels afterwards. Let's do that. See Smithson all together in a month. Find time, Annie. I *will* come and see you both, though, soon.'

There was the least hint of a pause.

'And I don't mean Christmas.'

They all three smiled then. A bond that held them was Mrs Avery's intransigence about Christmas. 'I did forty family Christmases,' she said (always), 'and I did every one myself without any help. I want no more. They depress me and they are dangerous. But I'd like to come and stay one night.'

There hung in the air a sort of resistance of which they were all ashamed.

But they kissed her almost affectionately at Annie's car, which had been left outside Mrs Avery's flat, as Mrs Avery refused to let them take her the three floors up to it.

'The climb is nothing to me,' she said as they all turned their faces up to its high windows.

'But can you do those stairs all right? We could give you a heave.'

'Of course I can. And I'm not going in yet. I need a walk on the common.'

'I suppose it's safe for you?'

'Well, I walk there every day of my life.'

'Keep to the edges then,' said Pete. 'It's a good rule.'

Annie and Pete got into the car and rolled down the windows and for a moment both faces stared ahead looking bleak, readjusting to the coming road, the rest of the day. 'Or searching for old feelings,' thought Mrs Avery, 'thinking how they have changed but that I am just the same. Quite wrong. They are feeling uneasy about me. For a moment. It will pass. All buried – until I am.'

Then she saw the two faces struggling after something. 'They are vulnerable,' she thought and noticed that Annie's hair had been coloured where it was going grey.

She watched Annie open a spectacle case and put glasses on her nose.

She looked at Pete's profile. The hairline was way back. 'Sardonic medallion,' she said.

'What?' he asked.

'I didn't speak.'

There were two deep vertical lines above the bridge of his nose, between his eyebrows, and she touched them. He flung away.

'You always did that,' she said.

'I dare say. You always said, "If you don't stop frowning they'll stay there." You said I was like the dog. Fixit had frown lines. "You're like the *dog*." You did say that to me, you know, Ma. That I was like the dog.'

'Well, I loved the dog, too.'

'That wasn't Fixit,' said Annie. 'It was Biddulph.' And quarrelling about dead dogs they drove off.

'Don't go too far,' they called. 'Don't get lost.'

'I'll ring,' called Pete. 'Sorry. Ghastly lunch. Be in touch. Pity.'

So she had decided to walk all the way to the blackberry bushes. She had walked past the pond, past the pub, past the château hotel again and over the cinder track. She had passed the last private houses on the edge of the golf course that stood like galleons breasting seas. She had passed the first green (this long walk had once been a car journey, when the children's legs were small) her lean old body tipping foward rather, her head down and her face sideways as if to escape a cold wind.

She had drawn her coat round her and felt pleasure. She still felt pleasure at having kept so elegantly slim. She put her old narrow feet down carefully, avoiding the rough.

She had passed through the scented broom, along beside the dry stream bed under the firs, and had come to the bramble patch with its comforting new seat.

She had sat.

She was not at all tired. Although she was not given to weeping, now, to her distaste, she wept.

She wept for her dead. Not for her husband, a shadowy man now, not for her mother any more, certainly not for her remote old father, dead when she was still at school. Not for old friends or old times. 'Not for my young body or my face,' she thought. 'Not for all the bright lust. Not for my childhood saints, my good ankles, my famous eyebrows ("like *accents circumflex*", some man had said; "like dear little tents", Annie had said when she was five). Not for my love affairs or my lost gods,' she thought. 'Just for my children. My dead children. I want them back.'

Out from the blackberry bushes the two came crawling. Annie's smocked dress all over juice. She saw Mrs Avery and looked frightened. She took Pete's hand and they stood together. 'I had forgotten the shape of his head,' she thought and the two old-fashioned children regarded Mrs Avery, who held out her hands.

'I know that dress,' she said to Annie. 'We never got the juice out.'

'It's her new one,' said Pete. 'You couldn't know it. Mum hasn't seen the juice yet.'

'I do,' said Mrs Avery. Now she held out her arms. 'I do know it. Oh, please come here.'

'No,' said Annie.

'We're not allowed,' said Pete.

'I could tell you a story.'

They wavered. 'It's all right,' said Pete, 'my mother's here. Just through the bushes. She tells us plenty of stories. She's just out of sight. She's lost the car keys and we have to go and help her. She's in a state already.'

Mrs Avery thought, 'I'd forgotten his knees and her straight parting.'

She heard her young cross voice calling and the children bobbed down and wriggled back through the bramble tunnel again. She concentrated, and then called out, 'They're by the car. You dropped them when you got out. Don't worry – you'll find them. You'll all get home. I promise, you'll all get home.'

Annie was dropping Pete off by Sloane Square and they sat in the car for a minute on the double yellow line waiting for the traffic to thin out enough for him to open his door.

'She's very well,' Pete said.

'Oh, she's fit enough. I hate the spots on the hands.'

'I wish she didn't fart.'

'Shut up. It happens. We'll do it. Both of us.'

'Oh, Christ!'

They sat on in the intimacy of a conversation impossible to hold with anyone but each other.

'Clueless about the money. As ever,' said Pete. 'Well – it may be years before we have to think what to do. She's eternal. Result of a boring life, I suppose. Awful life.'

'Awful day,' said Annie. 'The common looked good, though, didn't it? D'you remember the day we ran off and left her? When she lost the car keys? She was scattier then than she is now, when you come to think about it.'

'We were foul then.'

'No, we were easy,' said Annie. 'I know. I've had some.'

'D'you remember when we met that old bat on the common in the blackberries? She told us where Ma had dropped the car keys,' Pete said.

'I was scared of that woman. We never said anything about it. Not to each other, even.'

'We never even told Ma. Not anything. And we told her everything then. We did, you know. Well, anyway, I did!'

'I did too,' said Annie.

Pete looked down some tunnel. 'In the blackberry bushes,' he said. 'It was in the blackberry bushes. A nice old woman. About this time of year. God! – sometimes it seems about an hour ago.'

BEVIS

....

My cousin, Jilly Willis, a huge, leonine girl of nearly eighteen, arrived in the County Durham town where I had lived since I was born, with her mother, my Auntie Greta, and there was obviously something awful going on.

I knew it as soon as I stepped into the house from school. Something steamy. My mother stuck her head round the front room door and said, 'Tea in the kitchen. Can't come now.' This was unheard of.

My ma and Auntie Greta stayed shut in there together for hours. Jilly was not there. She must have been left behind at the boarding house where they'd taken rooms. I sat in the kitchen eating dried-up shepherd's pie. I could half hear their voices. On and on. Ma's brother, Auntie Greta's husband, Uncle Alec, had died two years before. He'd been an optician and worked over towards Northumberland where he'd met and married Auntie Greta and never once come back to see us. He had been a blameless man and when we at last met Auntie Greta we were silenced. At every meeting afterwards with her, we were silenced with renewed surprise. She was a fierce, raw-boned woman who never met your eye and always smiled. My mother could not speak of her, for she had come between her and her brother like a rough red wall.

★

Auntie Greta Willis and Jilly stayed on in our town after the day of the secret conversation and bought a little house over the sandhills that turned its back on everybody. They appeared to settle, and the following term Jilly started at my school. They hadn't sold their house in Northumberland because they'd left Auntie Greta's old mother in it. There seemed to be no shortage of money. Jilly was nearly six years older than I was and so at school I scarcely saw her. She was very clever. She had already been accepted on the strength of her A level examinations by the University of Edinburgh where she was to start next year in the Science faculty, and intended to become a vet. This last year at school was to fill in time and she had decided to do an extra A level in European History – 'To restore the balance,' her mother said. 'She won't do a year in Europe itself, like anyone else – they can't get her to shift.'

And I scarcely saw Jilly out of school either, though I think she came over to us with her mother sometimes for Sunday dinner. I sort of remember them being invited and all the rushing around after church to be ready for them. My mother and I were church-goers as Uncle Alec had been. He had been a great Christian and had sung in his church choir – ethereal Uncle Alec in his nervous metal specs. I don't suppose Jilly and her mother ever went to church with him. (My mother said, 'Ah, Jilly is a pagan lady.') I don't think that Auntie Greta ever went anywhere with him. When Uncle Alec died she wrote us a note long after the funeral and my ma wept for her brother as much as she had wept for my father. She said, 'Alec died of loneliness.'

★

'Why've they come here, Ma?'

'There's been a scandal.'

'What scandal?'

'I've sworn never to say.'

'Not even to me?'

'No. She made me promise that. Greta did. I'm very sorry.'

'Why did she?'

'Because you're only twelve.'

'Was it some sort of crime?'

'Not exactly.'

'I know. Jilly's been caught shoplifting.'

'No. Of course not.'

'People do when they're unhappy.'

'Rubbish,' said my mother. 'You didn't go shoplifting when your father died.'

When Jilly and her ma had been living near us for about six months, the abandoned grandmother fell ill and had to be put in a Home and while all this was being arranged by Auntie Willis, Jilly came to stay with us. She seemed very big. When the three of us sat down to meals in our tiny dining room she filled it like a doll in a box. Yet she was in no way gross, or out of proportion there. All she did was make us feel under-housed. She needed marble halls. She was a foreign body.

'One day,' my mother said, 'you'll be a magnficent Roman matron and you'll wear clothes that hang from the shoulder fastened by a barbaric clip.' Jilly looked startled, rather as if she had known this herself and had been keeping it private. My mother could often say things like this. Jilly looked sharp at my ma, and blushed. Jilly loved it. All of a sudden she was younger and sillier and began to go floating along to the bathroom at bedtime wrapped in a counterpane tied in a shoulder-knot, tossing her mane. 'Coliseo!' she cried and my ma cried, 'Imperatrix.' The house lightened. If only she could have stayed a little I think there might have been jokes. They were not quite in the air, but they were en route.

Her hair was bronzy and her mouth was proud. Her nose however was not Roman in the least but small, broad and flat like a lioness's and she had a lion's nobility about the brow. Her teeth when she smiled were small and white and square, like dice. Her eyes were not leonine but like her father's (said my ma), large and good and grey.

When Auntie Greta came back it was to tell us that the grandmother was very comfortable in the Home now, but failing, and had need of only one thing: a last visit from Jilly.

'We could wait,' the Aunt W said. 'I don't think it's that urgent. But then, you never know. It just might be. I can't go back – it's Bank Holiday and I'm on duty.' Auntie Greta was a nurse.

My ma said she was on duty then, too. Bank Holidays were her busiest times. She was a Samaritan.

'Well, I'm certainly not letting Jilly go on her own,' I heard the Willis say. 'Not by herself. Not next door again.'

'But haven't they all gone now?' asked Ma. 'There are new people next door now?'

'I'm not having her anywhere near. Not by herself. Not next door again even if it's empty.'

'Who's moved in there?'

'I've no idea and I don't want to know.'

'Couldn't she stay with the Chalmers? They were nice people. They were good friends to Alec. Before—'

'I'm afraid I never took to them at all.'

I'd been hanging about listening and they found themselves staring at me. Then they started coughing and pouring themselves more tea and behaving as though they'd been saying nothing at all. The Willis gave a sly look at her big bold palms. Ma said, 'I suppose you wouldn't like to go away for a weekend with Jilly, hinny? Back to her old home to see her gran in hospital? Stop her feeling homesick?'

'There'd be nobody else in the house,' said the Willis. 'You could do what you wanted, with Granny in the Gables. You could have plates on your knees and we haven't got rid of the telly yet. I'd maybe stand you a café tea.'

I went on painting my nails. I had my own friends and my own plans for Bank Holiday and I didn't believe that Jilly could still be homesick when I thought of the counterpane.

'Is that my nail varnish?' asked Ma.

'I'd soon put a stop to that,' said the Willis. 'I'd have given Jilly what-for for nail muck at thirteen.' She turned her empty teacup into the saucer to read the tea leaves.

You could see what her mouth would be like in old age. A draw-string purse tight shut. Everything was ingrowing with Greta. Her chest was concave below her great shoulders. I wondered if her breasts grew inwards too.

'I'm sure she'll go,' said Ma. 'Won't you, hinny? Because of Jilly's grandma – won't you?'

'Would Jilly want me?'

'She's easy,' said the Willis. 'There's one thing I'd ask though. You'd have to promise to keep near her. Keep close.'

'Oh, I'd be fine,' I said. 'I've been youth-hostelling by myself. I've been on a French exchange.' I'd hardly seen my French exchange as it happened though they didn't know it. I'd wandered all over Paris alone while Dominique sat looking *soignée* in bars, chain-smoking and behaving twenty-five. Her parents fortunately had made no enquiries about our views on the statues in the Louvre and my mother had not yet been made aware of the non-improvement in my French. That was to come.

'No,' said the W, 'what I mean is that you mustn't let Jilly go off alone. You mustn't leave her for a minute. See?' She was glaring at me like black ice.

'Is something the matter with Jilly?'

'She's not very well,' said Ma. 'Out of kilter. Out of true.'

'Teenage,' said the W and took out her handkerchief. She wiped her hands and dried off the corners of her mouth.

'Whatever did happen?' I asked when she'd gone.

'You'll have to tell me. It's not fair on me if you don't. Or safe. I shan't know the danger signals.'

'Oh, duck,' said Ma, 'oh, my hinny. I promised but I'll—'

'What?'

'I'll give you a—'

'Clue?'

'No. Not a clue. I promised. I'll give you a what's it? Example. Fable. Little story. Something I once saw and I've never forgotten.'

'Oh, Lord.'

'Listen. I was on the top of a tram once long ago. The tram had stopped in the middle of the road, as they did – as they do. It was when I was a student abroad somewhere. Standing on the pavement waiting for someone was a man. Reading a newspaper. He was old. Well, he seemed old to me. He may have been fifty or he may have been sixty – there's no difference when you're eighteen. The fact of him though was that he was most marvellously good-looking. I don't mean Byronic. Don Juanish. Flashy foreigner. He could have been from anywhere in the Western world. But he was a truly handsome man. I can still see him. "Beautiful" sounds soft, but, well – he was beautiful. There. I remember thinking, "Like a god. One of the old gods."

'Well, off the bus gets this girl and, hinny, she was plain! Not fascinating – ugly or quaint or arresting – just plain. Very, very ordinary, with thick glasses and lank hair and fat little bottle legs. She called out to the man and he looked up and dropped the newspaper on the pavement and smiled and held out his arms and she ran into them.'

'It was her father.'

'It was not her father.'

'How did you know?'

'I knew. It was huge, romantic love.'

'Oh, wow.'

'No. Not "oh, wow". Don't play tired-of-life at thirteen. It was love. They stood clasped together with people going round them as if they were a sculpture. Oblivious. After the tram started off again and swung round to the side at the end of the road I could still see them, still clasped together. And this was Italy. Maybe Holland. Not London. You'll know what that means one day.'

'So then?'

'So then, nothing. It just happened. So think.'

'Think what?'

'Think that there are some queer goings-on.'

I asked, 'Can we have the telly on now?' and Ma said, 'Oh, hin. I'm sorry. You're just a bairn. I've been asking a lot.'

'You mean making me go away with Jilly?'

'Yes,' she said, 'maybe that too.'

We went first to the Home and it smelled of mince. I said I'd wait for Jilly in the hall and she said, 'It's all right. I don't mind you coming in with me to see her, you know. It might even be better.'

'It's you she wants to see. I'd just fuddle her up.'

'Suit yourself,' she said. 'She won't exactly wave the flags when I walk in. That's just Mam. She never liked me and she hated Dad. Pass the mag. over.'

'Why can't you go on up now?'

'They said to wait. They're turning her. She's had a stroke. Didn't you know? You can come in with me. Are you frightened?'

'Why should I? She's not mine. Of course I'm not frightened.'

'Can you come now, dearie?' A fat lady had appeared round a cardboard wall that was pressed up against the banister of a coiled mahogany staircase that had once known crinolines. Hair sprouted about round her nurse's cap, pinned on crooked with hair slides. Whiskers stuck out of her chin and she was smoking. She looked more like an inmate than a nurse but that's England now, as Ma would say.

'I'll be outside,' I said.

'You can bring your friend. She won't mind.'

I fled and kicked the gravel outside until Jilly re-appeared, looking glassy. She hadn't been gone ten minutes. She said, 'We may as well walk on then, from here.'

We passed a pub called The Pit Laddie, and then a ramshackle bus passed us full of tired Indians. I said, 'What a lot of Indians all together,' and Jilly said, 'They're miners, fool. It's dirt. Haven't you been anywhere?'

We walked by the grand big clock-works of the coal face and up a steep cobbled street where women leaned against door frames scratching above their elbows. They looked golden Jilly up and down, saying nothing.

'Gran came from round this way,' she said.

'Did she know who you were?'

'She just looked. She rolled an eye about.'

'Did you talk to her?'

'Listen, shut up. I'll tell you one day when you're older. It's not important anyway.'

'You don't care about anybody, Jilly, do you? You don't care about a single human being.'

'Oh, no,' she said. 'Oh, most absolutely no. Miss Angel.'

We left the hilly strip streets and reached the ridge of the town above, where there was a new spread of small red houses and shops with the newfangled metal window frames. We came to other new houses built in groups and called after places in the Lake District: Derwent Crescent, Windermere Walk, Esthwaite Close. They were semi-dets, two and two, divided down the middle. The longer we walked the more money had been spent on lawn mowers, azaleas, plastic ponds, gnarled stumps of plastic trees. Gnomes fished. The last two houses were the finest, a low box hedge separating their gardens. On one side of it the grass was a foot high and full of weeds; on the other shorn and edged with metal strip. On the well-kept lawn a man crouched clipping precisely up to the middle of the hedge in a half knees-bend. Intently. Awkwardly. Snip, snip. Jilly wheeled towards the door of the scruffy house and opened the gate, which gave a cry. The man most carefully did not look at us but continued expertly snipping, then rose and went indoors.

Jilly produced a key and entered her old home which lay in semi-darkness and had an airless, old person's smell. She fell across a sofa and shut her eyes.

'What do we do now?' I asked after a bit. 'Jilly?'

'Suit yourself.'

Looking about I saw nothing that suited at all. The furniture of the whole house seemed to have been gathered into the room. A bed stuck out from a wall between a sideboard and a wardrobe. On a gummy, dusty dining-table stood pots of marmalade, packets of cornflakes and old library books. Burnt bread-and-milk stood black in a saucepan on the eau-de-nil lounge-tiles of the fireplace. Copper things on leather straps, ornamental bronze shovels, warming pans and a brass lady who wagged a bell-clapper under her skirts were reminders of more confident times. Uncle Alec's degree in ophthalmacy hung framed on a wall near a flight of flapping china ducks.

There was a knock on the front door.

'Mr Johnson just saw you as he was attending to the party hedge,' said the next-door Mrs. 'We just wondered if there was any news of Granny.'

'Oh,' I said, 'she's not mine. She's Jilly's.' I turned, but Jilly made signals with her arms, not opening her eyes.

'Anything we can do,' said Mrs Johnson, 'anything' – she tried to peer – 'we'd be glad. We've been so worried. We're only newcomers ourselves and we didn't want to impose. And we couldn't make her daughter hear when we rang the bell last week when she came to take her off. Granny got in a terrible state you know. We notified some mutual acquaintances, the Chalmers, and they were the ones sent out the alert to the daughter – that would be' (peering) 'your mother?'

Jilly was continuing to signal. 'Get rid of her. Close the door.'

'Of course it's the old next-door neighbours I blame,' said the woman. 'The people before us. They took no concern for her at all, no matter him being a Latin teacher at the comp. Useless stuff. And very stand-offish to all round about. Too good for this neighbourhood. Very well-to-do, though how I can't think on teacher's pay. Well, *she* had money. And a nice price they got out of us for the house and never a word about painted-over rotten window-sills. Hello, dear—'

Jilly had materialised beside me.

'Just the two of you here, alone? Well, that does seem a shame on your Bank Holiday.'

'We've been to the Gables to see my grandmother.'

'Well, I'm very glad. I am glad. I've just been saying to your sister—'

'Cousin.'

'Sorry, dear, cousin – I've just been saying— Could I just step inside? Oh, dear – that pan. And all those grease marks round the chair. That'll bring mice. I was saying, I blame the neighbours before. The people before us. They could have found out who to contact. We knew nobody crescent-wise and they'd been here for years. Just as you had, dear. Born here, weren't you? Very cold people you had next door. Southerners I dare say and always away foreign. Would you both like a bite of something?'

'No thanks,' I said. 'We've been told to go to the Chalmers.'

'Actually, yes. We would,' said Jilly. 'Thanks, we would.'

'Half an hour then? Give me time to make things nice.'

★

'I don't want to go,' I said. 'Why ever did you say we'd go? We could have had chips.'

'Or gone to the charming Chalmers like Mummy said, little lambkin.'

'No – I don't want to go to the Chalmers.' (I was shy with the Chalmers. They sent big presents at Christmas and I never could get my thank-you letters to sound grateful enough. They were gods in the shadows.) 'I just don't want to go in next door. They're busybodies. And if they'd really cared about your gran they wouldn't have let her eat out of pans.'

'You didn't know my gran,' said Jilly. 'No,' she said. 'We'll go. We may as well. There'll be hot water and they might let us have a bath. Everything's switched off here.'

'Your mother isn't a very good organiser, is she?'

'Well, she's not all over you all the time and she's kept her figure.'

Cold at heart – for I was a retarded thirteen and still believed that all other girls were jealous of me because my mother was so incomparably better than theirs – I spoke not one word as I followed Jilly up the tidy side of the hedge towards Mr Johnson, who was holding open his front door and looking down at the path in order not to see Jilly's legs.

Inside the door, what should have been the mirror image of Jilly's house was frighteningly different. A forest of new chairs in Jacobean print stood on high-glaze parquet and all was open-plan behind slatted rainbow blinds. 'We had to do a great deal of work here,' said Mrs

Johnson. 'A lot of knocking through. The last people –
well, it hadn't been changed since the war. Finger plates
above the door knobs with Greek ladies carrying jars of
irises and daffodils in plaster-work round the lounge
fireplace. And little bits of stained glass. It was a scream.'

'We're told it was an intellectual family,' said Mr
Johnson, *Readers' Digest* open by his plate. He seemed
troubled by something and put his serviette to his face
and smelled it.

'It's my scent,' said Jilly, not looking at him.

'The man before – the teacher – he'd had foreign
education and a varsity degree,' said Mrs Johnson.

'Oh, yes, it's a good neighbourhood,' continued Mr
Johnson. 'I wonder if your mother has had any thought
yet – could you ask her? – about the selling of the house,
strokes being what they are. Naturally it affects us.
Pricewise the right people will be important in the
crescent. One has to take an interest.'

'Could I go upstairs?'

They looked surprised. Jilly was two bites into her fish
pie. Mrs J said, 'Of course, dear. First on the left.'

'I know.'

She disappeared up the spiral staircase for what seemed
hours. The Johnsons were uneasy. They talked on
brightly but appeared to be listening. I wondered what
they'd heard about Jilly and again I had the random
thought about stealing. Why did I always come back to
the thought of Jilly as a taker? A danger? A foreigner
among us all?

She was back, looming above us over the white
wrought iron. She looked flushed. 'Mr Johnson,' she

said, 'could I ask you for something very special? A very special favour? A loan?'

He turned pink through his light moustache, 'Of course my d—'

'Have you a bike? Could we borrow a bike for tomorrow? We don't have to be home before evening and we can't spend the whole day sitting with Gran.'

There was a fractional hesitation before Mr Johnson said, 'Yes,' and Mrs Johnson said, 'I'm afraid Mr Johnson only has his racing bikes. He's been a professional, you know. Connected with the Luton Twelve.'

'We'd take great care of it.'

'Yes. Yes, of course,' said Mr Johnson.

After supper he brought ticking through the house a flimsy fine-drawn grasshopper with slim crossbar and saddle like a whippet.

'Twenty-seven ounces,' he said. 'Hero of the Luton Twelve.'

'*And* the Bedford Four,' said Mrs Johnson.

Mr Johnson was stroking the saddle and looking at Jilly's legs, starting low, gliding upwards. 'Do you think you can manage it?'

'Oh, it's not for me, it's for her,' Jilly said looking straight at him and smiling. 'Mine's still in Gran's shed. Don't worry, my cousin's a terrific rider.'

'But I've never—'

'You are very kind,' – she looked at him again – 'we'll take the greatest care of it.'

'Would you like a practice run?' asked Mr J as we left, looking at my legs quite differently, finding them unreassuring.

'Oh, she's terribly good,' said Jilly.

In the Gran's house I said, 'You're awful, Jilly. You're deceitful. You're mad, too. I can't ride a bike like that.'

'We'll have a dummy run first thing tomorrow. You'll be OK.'

'*You* can ride it.'

'I can't ride it. I'm far too heavy. I can just cope with my own and it's like a sofa. We'll get up early. We'll go to bed now.'

In the morning we wheeled the two bikes respectfully away from Wastwater Crescent and down the cobbled hill to the Gables.

'You keep going round the gravel till I'm out,' Jilly said, and when she came back I was tottering in zigzags, heading for easy jumping-off places, but making a little progress.

'How is she?'

'She's a lot better. They've been feeding her gravy.'

'*Gravy?*'

'She likes gravy. Don't look like that. She always liked it. She slurped it up with a spoon. She used to fill up her Yorkshire puddings with it, like a pond, and it used to spill out all over her great bits of beef. She liked her beef leathery like tongues in shoes. She used to slap her lips, slap, slap. She dribbled. She always dribbled. Her mouth perpetually watered. She was always foul.

'Don't look so saint-like,' she said. 'There are horrible people and I hate her.'

We pushed the bikes up cobblestone slopes of little houses and soon came out to open country with high blue hills along the horizon, and a great sky. Clouds rolled over it like tumbleweed in Westerns.

'She used to beat me.'

'*What!*'

'My gran. She called it "leathering". She used to leather me with a belt. Grow up.'

'But your *mother* was there!'

'She'd been leathered by her, too. Sometimes they both leathered me together. What's the matter? D'you want me to help you up on the bike? Why've you gone white?'

'But your *mother*! She was married to Uncle Alex. My mother's own brother.'

'Oh, Dad used to turn white, too. He used to go and sit in the shed while it was going on. I used to scream. It was when I was little.'

'Shut up, shut up, shut up.'

'It's all right. Dad's dead. He was weak. *Il souffre* but *il est mort*. Gran soon will be, thank God. I don't give a toss for her. Or my mother.'

'But, Jilly, there's always a reason for wickedness. *Jilly!*'

She leapt on the lumbering bike and began to push the pedals down, one-two, with her strong legs until she was away over the hill. After an unpromising start and a fall or two on the lonely road I clenched my teeth and got the hang of it. Soon I was understanding the gears.

I came up alongside Jilly and flew past her. I stopped, one foot on a boulder, balancing with my hand against the stony wall that accompanied us over the moor like a snake, westward towards the Irish Sea.

'Wherever are we going, Jilly?'

She was heaving her bike up the hill towards me, one leg pressing down, then the other, head turning left and then right.

She was like a solemn giant, slowly dancing.

'We're going to his new house. I'm going to see him again.'

'Whose house?'

'Use your empty head. Our old neighbours'.'

'D'you know the address?'

'Yes. He told me it. Before we left he managed to get a note to me – God knows how, but he's brilliant. We both knew – we'd always known – I'd have to go the minute they found out. It was a matter of time. We knew that. One of us would have to move. I'd pretty well finished at the comp. It was his comp too, but – well, we knew of course it'd have to be me.'

'Jilly – what happened?'

'Do you honestly not know?'

And I did know of course. In the cradle, at the breast, probably in the womb we know. When they announce what they call the facts of life they are never really a surprise.

'No, I don't,' I shouted as she pedalled on past me and away towards the purple, banked-up clouds ahead.

'How far is it, Jilly? How far?'

I caught her up and began to weave about around her and then diagonally in front of her, across and across the road.

'Jilly? Jilly, can we stop and have the chocolate? Jilly?'

On she went, and passed me.

'Not far now,' she called as the first big drops fell and the wind began. 'Bloody cold,' she called.

'Where are we *going*? There aren't any houses up here. It's mad. I'm going back.'

'Fine. Go.'

'I promised not to leave you.'

'In case what? Did they say why? In case I went off with him? In case I got kidnapped by him?'

'I don't know what you're talking about, Jilly. Honestly. I don't.'

The rain had become cold and soaking by the time we had climbed the next long hill, Jilly plugging up it slower and slower but never giving up, never getting off to walk. I'd been pushing my bike for some time already. It was so light that I had to walk beside it to hold it down. It was trying to blow away over the wall into the heather.

To the north of our walled road I saw a blacker, higher, more organic-looking ridge squirming out of sight. It looked as old as the rock.

'Whatever is it, Jilly?'

'Roman Wall. We're nearly there.'

'Roman this, Roman that. *Jilly*!' Mother going on about Jilly belonging to another country. I had an exhausted, frightened knowledge that she was pedalling me away to it, and out of time – I didn't know whether forward or backward. But I did know where she was going wasn't for me.

She seemed to be almost flying ahead now and the rain flung itself on the shiny, lilac road and the wind struck me in the face. There was a great space of empty moor all round, not a building not a signpost.

'Jilly!'

I saw her ahead, turning left, south, down a dirt track, out of sight, and I followed her, bumping over stones into a dip, out of a dip, then as we climbed again one behind the other we were all at once beside a long metal field gate standing wide open. Just inside and to the right was a tin-roofed Dutch barn and across what once had been an old Northumbrian farmyard but now had flowers planted in its horsetrough was a spruced-up farmhouse painted glittering white. Two stables now fitted with metal up-and-over garage doors stood near. An ornamental wagon wheel, also painted white, was arranged beside an old pump made to look fancy and the start of a sparse rockery on what had been a midden. No sign of an animal; not a cat, not a chicken, and not one weed in the shining cobbles. I saw all this only after we had both collapsed inside the open-sided barn and could look out at it through rain that fell like silver arrows. Jilly let her bike drop and went round a corner, to sit on a hayblock, knees apart, hands clasped, bowing her wet head. Her hair was plastered against her skull, dark and dripping, as I suppose was mine.

'Jilly?'

I burrowed about, pulling at the hay, trying to get some loose to put it round me like bedclothes. Before us was a great view of sky and moor, the cocky, ravished farmhouse behind. Through the rain, toward the road I saw some flashes of light, like swords, far away. Then the sky cleared, the flashes vanished and the sun came out with ice-cold raindrops still striking down from the clouds blown away, like light from dead stars. The view, sopped with rain, dazzled. Sunlight caught a distant bracelet of Roman Wall, then left it.

'They must have had days like this,' I said.

'Who must?'

'The Romans.'

She said nothing.

I said, 'They must have got ever so depressed. So cold. So far from Italy and nobody talking Latin.'

'They'd been here long enough,' she said, 'they'd probably forgotten Latin. They'd have talked pidgin English – chop chop and doolally and that. It was like home here. Well, all Europe was home then. Anyway, they were soldiers, weren't they? They were used to it. It's the girls back home you've to be sorry for – left behind with the wimps. They were the ones to be depressed.'

It was nice she was thinking of all this instead of—

'Jilly,' I said, 'let's go back. This place is empty. They're all away. They'll be away for Bank Holiday.'

'Yes.' Her voice was dead.

After a while she said, 'They'll be at the boat.'

'Boat?'

'They've a boat. They have everything. Been everywhere. He has everything. Everything in the world that life can give.'

'He hasn't got you Jilly. I bet he misses you.'

She leaned over to her bike and burrowed in the saddlebag and brought out a notebook and a pencil and scribbled something.

'Jilly. Jilly – what's his name?'

'Bevis.'

'*Bevis*.'

'Yes,' she said. '*Bevis*. Why not?'

'I don't know. It's a bit—'

'It's Latinate,' she said. Solemnly.

Our eyes met across the hay. And held. '*Bevis*!'

Held unblinking.

I had the extraordinary notion that the gods were assembled and were on my side. I might save Jilly now.

'It's a family name,' she said with hauteur.

I said, 'Coo-er!'

Her lips and nose for a lovely instant twitched. But then – 'And what may I ask does that mean, po-face?'

'Well, isn't it – a bit sort of comic?'

'*Comic*?' Oh, very proud. Swallowing. Tossing back the lion's drying mane. Glaring down the lion's flat nose.

'Well, you know. It sounds like some sort of bread.'

'*Bread*?'

'Or some sort of beverage. A sort of wheat-germ drink.'

'*Beverage*!'

Our eyes held steady and then hers flickered and her mouth trembled and I thought, I've done it!

But no.

She turned her head and sank sideways in the hay and the wind kicked the tin roof of the barn about and clattered it like a thundersheet. With plumes of water at its wheels a long car with a boat behind it on a trolley came rollicking down the track from the moor and swept through the farm gate. A great many people shot out of the car and disappeared into the house.

Jilly did not stir.

'Jilly, they're back. The family's back.'

Now down the lane came the flashes I had seen before, far off, a group of cyclists in shiny black-beetle capes, peaked caps and bikes as ritzy as mine. In the tracks of the car they swooped into the yard and over to the barn and dismounted all around us, wet through. Ignoring us, they shook themselves like dogs, began removing their capes and mopping their streaming faces. 'She all right?' one of them asked, nodding towards Jilly.

'Yes. She's just tired.'

'Wild day,' said another. 'How far you come? That's a nice bike.'

'I'm just borrowing it. It belongs to someone to do with the Luton Twelve.'

'You coming in with us?'

'In?'

'The house. The geezer in the car said to go in and get dry.'

'But it's stopped raining almost now.'

'Yeah. Look bad though not to go in. After he said.'

They were skinny little people with faces narrowed by continuous slipstream, eyes sharp like birds' eyes, sinews like cords. Under their capes they wore brilliant, proud colours – orange and scarlet and green. Motley, international people. 'Come on. You come on in too.'

They made off towards the farmhouse.

'Shall I?' I went over to Jilly as she sat with her back to me. 'Shall I go in with them, Jilly?'

All she did was pass me the note she'd written. On the outside of it she'd scrawled 'Bevis', the tail of the S curled down like a tendril and crossed at the end with a kiss.

'Read it if you like.'

'No. I don't.'

'Read it. I mean it. Give it to him. He'll know it the minute he sees it. I used to leave one for him like this every day. In the rabbit hutches. Until they found one.'

I read it. It said, 'I'm in the hay barn – Jilly.'

'Give it to him, go on. You'll be too late.'

Someone had in fact already shut the front door behind the last of the cyclists when I reached it and I had to bang hard and at once or I should have faltered. It was immediately opened by a fiftyish sort of man who stood smiling at me. He was shortish, squarish and older than Dad had been but there was a sweet, calm presence all around him as he looked down affectionately at me as I stood soaked through and silent at his door.

'Hullo. One more. Come in. Come in. We're just back from the sea and you look as though you've been in it.' He stood back to let me pass down the flagstones, wetted ahead of me by all the cyclists' feet.

'Come along, through, my dear. Get warm. There'll be a fire in a minute but come and stand by the stove first. Are you the last of them?' He peered across the yard.

I couldn't stop looking at him. For the first time since I was a child I wanted to reach out and touch someone. I remembered the feel of my father's clothes again. Such strength, such kindness. Good heavens – old, *old*. And yet I could see the comfort of his arms folding themselves round damaged Jilly. I saw her beautiful head on his shoulder in the house with the Grecian ladies engraved upon the finger plates; and the fireplaces traced with daffodils.

Then his wife came up alongside and put a hand on his arm. She was a square woman, short, with wiry hair. She was powerful. As powerful as Caesar's wife, as powerful as Volumnia. Her eyes shone. 'Excuse me, dear,' she said to me, and then to him, 'Come in quickly. Great news. *Great* news,' and a sound came floating from a room down the passage that made one think of goals being scored and tides of applause. A wimpish boy and a solid girl came forward flapping letters and the girl flung herself upon her father who swung her round and then put his arm round the boy as well. He hugged both his children together.

'*Well*!' said Volumnia to everyone, and the cyclists all gazed. 'Well, we've come home in style. It's the examination results and we have two heroes. *Heroes*!' She shone with such pride she looked beautiful.

'On the mat,' the boy shouted, waving the letter. 'On the mat. I knew they'd be waiting on the mat. And there they were – yooh, yooh.' The girl was giving long silly shrieks and had laid herself along a window seat.

'What they on about?' one of the cyclists asked me and I said, 'She's happy. Some girls at school do it.'

'Straight A's,' said the lovely father. 'Straight A's for both of them. Two people climbing to the top of the tree. Right to the top. And all set fair.'

The boy grinning with happiness came loping across to me. 'D'you want a towel? Are you cold? D'you want some cocoa?' But all he meant was 'For me the whole world is set fair.' The girl went on squealing.

And the sun came out and splashed the wet landscape while the rain still attacked the windows of the house with occasional showers of arrows, as if some ancient little army were bitterly out on the moor. Volumnia led us all to a table in another room and put a bowl of soup in front of each of us as she smiled and smiled. There was nothing, nothing, she would not do today, wrapping us all into her magnificent family, for whom all was set fair.

'Shall I relieve you of that?' I heard his voice say over my shoulder as he leaned forward to put a bread basket on the table. My wrists had been propped on the table edge while I waited to see if we were meant to start in on the soup. My left hand had been holding the note marked 'Bevis', with its kiss. The note was no longer there. It had been tweaked away.

Everyone was talking and laughing, gobbling soup and bread, and the cyclist next to me was saying, 'Did you say you were something to do with the Luton Twelve? I'm really more interested in the Bedford Four.'

And Jilly was in the hay barn. Would Bevis go out to her — oh, would he go?

I said, 'Excuse me,' to the cyclist, slid off my chair and went over towards the kitchen where I saw the man standing gravely beside the stove, with the note. He looked up, not towards me standing outside the door but at the big fat bottom of his wife as she bent to the refrigerator: her old back, her grey wire hair. Then, when she straightened up and turned to him, he did the thing that ended everything. He lifted the note and held it out to her.

She put down whatever it was she'd been looking for in the fridge. I think it was cheese. A great slab of heavy cheese. She walked towards him, took the note and read it, then they looked hard at each other. The man then touched her shoulder, lifted off the little round lid of the stove by its iron handle, took the note back from her hand and dropped it down in the hot coals. She took his hand and held it against her face and they both smiled.

'Jilly. Jilly – where are you?'

She had scarcely moved.

'Jilly, we've got to go. We'll be late. For the train. It's miles and miles.'

'You've gone white again. Did you give Bevis the note?'

'Yes.'

'Well?'

'I don't know. Jilly – let's go. Why are we sitting in this barn? Jilly – you don't want to get pneumonia.'

'I'm not leaving till I've seen him. He'll come out in a minute.'

'He won't. No – don't look at me. He won't.'

'He read it?'

'Yes, he read it.'

'And?'

'Jilly, I want to go home.'

'Not,' she said, gripping my wrist and I saw for the first time that she had hands not unlike Auntie Greta's, 'not till you tell me.'

'He threw it in the stove.'

'So that they wouldn't see it?'

'No. She was there. Let go. She saw it, too. She read it, too. They—'

'Yes?' She flung away my wrist and stood up from the

hay and the over-large landscape behind looked perfectly right for her. 'Yes?'

'They put it in the stove together. Then they smiled.'

An age later she said lightly, 'Oh, well.'

'OK,' she said, 'never mind. So what?'

It frightened me more than anything.

'If you like we could wait a bit, Jilly.'

'No,' she said. 'No, I don't think so.'

Her carthorse sped ahead of my racehorse over the wide terrain. Along the wet purple road we flew, paced to the north by the frontier of the Wall, over moors and hills and dykes and ditches, and back to the present-day country of pits and little houses and hedges and shrubs. 'You'd better dry his bike,' she said.

Mr Johnson came out of his house and she undid him with her smile. 'We're just going to dry your lovely bike.'

'Oh, that's all right. I'll see to it. Not necessary at all.'

His blush was dark as potted meat. He pleaded with her for some sign.

None.

Half an hour and we were gone.

Because the Bank Holiday was not over until the following day the train home was practically empty and we sat silent in it as far as Sunderland, a stygian place the train enters and leaves through a black tunnel (like life, quoth the preacher) and where Jilly got out and disappeared. She returned, not hurrying – I had been in terror for she had the tickets and the money and knew where we had to change trains – with a big bag of crisps. She ate the crisps slowly giving none to me, staring out of the window. We were alone until Middlesbrough.

Then she said, still staring out, 'Ever been had?'

'Had?'

'Had.'

'You mean, made to look silly? Yes. All the time. Oh, Jilly!'

'Had, had, had, *had*,' she said. '*Had*, Miss No-Secrets Angel. You know perfectly well what I mean.'

'You mean – kissing?'

'*Had*,' she said. 'You know. He *had* me. He had me and had me and had me. Every morning in his bed for weeks and weeks and weeks. He HAD me. And how did he have me, Angel Po-Face? How did he have me? Let me count the ways. He begged me and begged me and so in the end I climbed out of my bedroom and into his bedroom next door. Every morning at five o'clock and back at seven and down eating breakfast with Gran and Mam, and then walking down the path either side of that fond hedge – three of them and one of me, and off to the comp by eight all together. We never said a word in the car.'

'But I can't see how. Did he have a bedroom alone then?'

'Yes, he had a bedroom alone. Don't you know anything yet?'

I thought, 'I suppose not. I don't. I don't understand anything at all.' It must be because there aren't any men in our house. I didn't know that men don't always sleep with their wives.

'Jilly. Wasn't it—? Weren't you scared?'

'Getting pregnant? No. I don't know why. He didn't use anything. Why've you got your hands over your ears? Take them away. Listen. You have to grow up sometime.'

I said, 'Sorry,' but I didn't know what I meant.

'And God was I tired,' she said when we stopped at Cargo Fleet siding. 'Was I tired at school. But I got an A in every subject. My mind was as clear—

'Oh, God,' she said, staring at the steelworks through the rain, 'I was so happy.'

At Warrenby some people got into the carriage and I sat looking at the floor. I heard one of them say to Jilly – righteously, fiercely, like Teesside people do – 'What's your little sister crying for?' but Jilly didn't answer.

'One thing, I suppose,' she said to me the following week at school – it was the day before she left; she'd failed the History. 'One thing—' She had come up behind me in the dark part of the corridor outside the science rooms and caught hold of the back of my tunic. She twisted it and the knickers underneath till it hurt, 'I suppose you didn't see anything in him, did you? You thought he was nothing. You thought "Who could see anything in that little shit?" '

'Oh, let go, Jilly.'

'Don't cry,' she said. 'You're always crying.'

I was crying because I'd expected love to be beautiful but I didn't say so.

'Come on then,' she said, 'let's hear it. What did you think of him?'

I said, 'He was wonderful.'

Jilly died at forty-two, suddenly, in Rome. A brain haemorrhage. Something flicked across a lifeline and she was gone. She had not become a vet. She had not even gone to university. She had gone off on her own at the end of the summer term of the Bank Holiday; first to Paris, where she had become a model for a time. Later she took up with a famous Italian photographer and became a beautiful, known face. There were a few films and then one lavish one that for a short moment gave her face to the whole world. The tawny hair blew out beside autostradas and autoroutes and freeways. The grey eyes stared down at Eros in Piccadilly, at the Corso in Rome, the dust of Athens and the severity of Madrid. But soon it was gone.

Later one kept seeing her in hairdressers' society magazines, always with what is called 'the international set', which is to say with those whose names are known only to each other, like cyclists but corrupting. There was a nasty divorce and some hard publicity about money and lovers. But it was not a louche life. If anything, I believe it was rather a dry one. She never grew druggy or raddled or mean, and always her face stayed right.

She never came back.

For a while her mother hung about our town but then without warning she moved away too and we heard of her no more. Sometimes my mother said, 'I feel rather bad about Greta. She *is* my sister-in-law. I suppose we could find her. But she never cared for us. And she left no address.'

But Jilly and I kept in touch always. We wrote at least six times a year and I heard from her the week before she died. I miss her great scrawl, the fat letters with the foreign stamps, heavy on the mat, although they never really said much.

She died just a month before the Chalmers' grandchild's wedding, to which our whole family had been invited, very generously, I thought, since we hadn't seen any of them for years. Off we set – my mother and stepfather, me, my husband and my children in a couple of cars, and very glad to be together for as my mother said, 'There won't be a soul there we recognise except them and maybe not even them'.

'And the *place*!' she said. 'Just look. Oh, poor Alec – look. All the cobbles have gone. D'you remember all the women on the doorsteps? And the pit-heads and the coal dust?'

Up the slope where we had pushed the bikes between the grim little houses there was only wasteland and ruin, boards over windows and notices saying 'Demolition'. The Lake District crescents were looking shabby though I thought I saw the box hedge. Only the Chalmers' house, the old rectory over the hill, was bravely surviving beside the unchanged church.

A marquee had been put up on the lawn, approached through the house and the old rector's study. Sensible coconut matting led to the line-up of the bride and groom.

And just beyond this I found myself head on to Mr and Mrs Johnson, looking little changed. They were smiling nervily over their champagne glasses, looking this way and that for a familiar face and seemed delighted with me out of all proportion. They swooped forward.

'No, I'm afraid we don't—' Tense wide smiles.

'You hardly would. I was just thirteen. I borrowed your racing bike, Mr Johnson. I was with my cousin, Jilly Willis.'

They almost took bites out of me. '*Remember*!' they said. 'Remember – of course we do. Remember! *What* a lovely girl!'

'We saw the obituaries,' said Mrs Johnson. Mr Johnson said, 'Tragic. And so young. It was a great mistake for her to travel.

'The way she swept off on the bike and never on a racing bike before. Amazing.

'I often boast about it,' said Mr J; 'that Jilly Willis once borrowed one of my bikes. I still have it hung up in the shed by the old hutches. Out of sentiment for her – and of course for my time with the Luton Twelve.'

'And the Bedford Four,' said his wife.

I introduced them to my mother and heard them saying that of course they understood that we were not relations of the grandmother. Not *blood* relations.

Looking down I found myself staring at the wiry and unthinning hair of Volumnia.

She filled her chair and sat in it as if it were a throne, but there were two sticks and elbow-pieces propped beside her and her feet were swollen round the shoestraps. She was dancing a small child on her knee.

'Hullo,' she said, looking up at me. 'Now, who are you? I'm afraid I'm rather blind but I know you, don't I? I remember you, I think.'

'You couldn't,' I said. 'We met when I was almost a child and now I'm nearly forty. But I recognise you. We met at your house in the wilds, one wet Bank Holiday.'

'Oh, *that* house,' she said. 'My word, that *was* a romantic house. Very silly. It didn't last long, I'm afraid. Too far out. You must have been a friend of the children – my dear, they're both here. The twins. Both behind you.'

Two indeterminate people were laughing nearby and the one who had been the drippish boy looked round – chinless, red-lipped, white-eyelashed. I remembered him at once.

'He became a vet. I expect you know?' said his mother. 'Doing so well.'

'The day we met he had just passed all his O levels. It was a very wild, haunted sort of day.'

'Really?' You could see she thought little of the adjective. 'But how curious—' Then she stopped.

'I came in to shelter. I was with my cousin, Jilly Willis. I was with some cyclists. I was Jilly Willis's cousin.'

She looked down at the grandchild on her knee. She bounced him up and down. 'There we are,' she sang, 'there we are.'

'I expect you remember Jilly?'

'That's my baby. Baby boy. Yes, I remember Jilly Willis very well.'

'So do I,' said the son joining us, wineglass tipping rather. 'Hullo. Who are you? Ought I to know you?'

'I'm Jilly's cousin.'

'I knew Jilly from being a baby,' he said. 'Bloody sad. So young. She was only a few years older than me, you know. We kept rabbits together. It was Jilly started me off wanting to be a vet.' His glass was refilled and he drank. 'Started me off on a lot of things as a matter of fact. Between ourselves.'

'Diddle-dee-dee,' sang Volumnia to the baby, 'Bevis, Bevis, Bevis-boy.'

'Is your father here?'

'I'm afraid my father's dead,' he said. 'Do you remember him? Really? Great. Oh – super chap. Lovely man. We miss him.' He drained the glass again.

' "Bevis",' I said and saw the sweet-tempered face and Jilly's eyes enlarge with love at the sound of the name. Jilly refusing to mock.

'Yes, Bevis,' he said. 'It's a family name. My son's name.'

'And it was your father's name,' I said.

'Actually, no. No it wasn't. Dad missed out on Bevis for some reason. He was Rodney. No – I'm Bevis.'

TELEGONY

....

I: Going into a Dark House

Molly Fielding's mother had been a terrible woman born about the same time as Tennyson's Maud and as unapproachable.

Nobody knew anything much about her, Molly herself being now very ancient. Molly had been my grandmother's friend and my mother's, before she was mine, but with the demise of each generation she seemed to grow younger and freer – to take strength. Her hair, her clothes, her house, all were up to the minute. So were her investments; and her foreign holidays became farther and farther flung.

I had found the photograph of her mother before my own mother died. It was a coffee-coloured thing mounted on thick, fluffy, cream paper, unframed in a drawer, with the photographer's name in beautiful copperplate across the corner: 'Settimo'.

I could not believe it. Signor Settimo! He had taken my own photograph when I was a child. I remembered a delicious little man like a chocolate, with black hair and eyes and Hitler's square moustache. My Settimo must have been the son – or even grandson – of course. Molly Fielding's mother must have known the first. Probably the first Settimo had come over from Italy with the ice-cream makers and organ grinders of the *fin de siècle*. It was a long-established firm when I knew it and a photographer in the English Midlands with a glamorous, lucky name such as *Settimo* would be almost home and dry. All he'd need would be flair and a camera and a book of instructions – a match for anyone.

But not for Molly Fielding's mother. Oh, dear me no. There she sits, her strong jaw raised, its tip pointing straight at the lens. Very watchful. She is examining the long hump of Mr Settimo beneath the black cloth behind the tripod. Her eyes – small eyes – are saying, 'Try – but you'll not take me. *I* take.'

Her great face, like his small one, is covered in black cloth. Hers is covered by a fine veil of silk netting, tied tight round the back of her neck by a broad black velvet ribbon. It is stitched at the top round the hat brim – a tight hat, expensive and showy, glittering with jet beads like the head of a snake. Her own head is proudly up, her eyes are very cunning. Oho, how she despises Mr Settimo, the tradesman. She is smiling a most self-satisfied smile. She is armed with a cuirass of necklaces across her beaded front, a palisade of brooches, great gauntlets of rings. She is fair-skinned beneath the veil. She must have been a pretty young girl, and her mouth, above the chin grown fierce, is still small and curly and sexy. No lady. Like somebody's cook but in the way that duchesses can look like somebody's cook. Not born rich, you can see – but now she *is* rich. At this moment, seated before foreign little Mr Settimo, she is rich. I never saw a nastier piece of work than Molly

Fielding's mother. I swear it. I don't know how I knew – but I swear it.

'What an awful woman. Who is it?'

My mother said, 'Oh, dear, that's old Molly Fielding's mother. I knew her. She was a character.'

'You *knew* her! She looks before the Punic Wars.'

'She was, just about. God knows. An authentic mid-Victorian. She had Molly very late. She was famous for some sort of reputation but I can't remember what it was. She died about the time Molly married, and that would be all of sixty years ago.'

'What was the husband like?'

'Oh, long gone. Nobody knew him. Molly can't remember him. Maybe there wasn't a husband, but I think I'd have remembered if it was that. I think he was just dispensed with somehow. He was very weak – or silly. But rich.'

'She doesn't look as if she would have needed anyone, ever.'

'Well, she certainly didn't need poor old Molly. Her only child, you know, and she hated her. Molly – such a silent little thing at school. After that she was "at home with mother".'

'Didn't she ever work?'

'Are you mad, child? She had to gather up her mother's shawls and go visiting with her and return the library books.'

'Until she married?'

'Yes. And she'd never have married if her mother could have stopped it. She was always very attractive,

Molly. Not beautiful but attractive. She was never let out of her mother's sight – and not let into anyone else's. They lived in hotels, I think, up and down the country. Sometimes in boarding-house places abroad. There had been a big house somewhere but they left it!'

'Were they poor?'

'Rich, dear, rich. Just look some time at Molly's rings.'

This conversation was years ago and since then I have often looked at Molly's rings. I looked at them the other day when she came to lunch with me and they still shone wickedly, catching the light of the winter dining room, weighting down her little claws. Molly was a trim, spare, little woman and the claws were smaller now and even sharper-looking than when I'd seen her last, two years ago. Her nails were tiny and beautifully manicured and the prickly old clusters below them looked loose enough at any moment to go sliding off into the chicken supreme.

'Looking at the rings?' she asked. 'You're not getting them, dear. They're for impeccable Alice. My albatrosses. She could have them now if she wanted. I hardly wear them. High days and holidays, like this. I keep them in – no, I'm not going to tell you. You never know. Careless talk . . . You think they're vulgar, do you?'

'No. I was just – well, remembering them. From way back. They looked smaller then. Your rings were you. Most things look bigger when you're young.'

'I'm smaller,' she said, 'that's all it is. I keep getting them re-made but they can't keep pace with me. I get them done over every year before the insurance runs out.

138

I tell the insurance people the stones rattle. They don't, but you can get them cleaned free if you say that. A jeweller cleans them better than you can yourself. A good jeweller always cleans when he secures. Gin – that's all you can do for yourself, soak them in gin. But it's a waste. You feel you can't drink it afterwards with all the gunge in it.'

The rings shone clear and sharp and there was not a trace of gunge and never had been, for Molly had a code of practice for the maintenance of goods that would have impressed a shipping company; and she had an eye for the free acquisition of necessities and schemes for the painless saving of money that many a government might envy. She also had a talent for the command of luxury. Stories of Molly sharing hotel rooms for which her friends and acquaintances had paid were in my childhood canon. She had slept on the floor of the Hyde Park, for instance, with her daughter's old nanny who had struck it rich with a (now absent) South American lover.

'Nanny had the bed of course – I insisted. Yes, she did fuss about me being on the floor, and we did change over about eleven o'clock, but I'd have been perfectly happy. Who minds sleeping on a floor if it saves two hundred pounds a night? They never notice, you know. I'd been Nanny's dinner guest and we went up to her room after dinner as if to get my coat. No one notices if you don't go home. And it was Harvey Nichols' sale in the morning, just across the road. I felt since I'd saved two hundred pounds I could spend it.'

'But, Molly, you didn't *have* to spend two hundred pounds. You didn't *have* to go in to London the night before at all. You only live in Rickmansworth.'

'Oh, but there's nothing in Rickmansworth like the Hyde Park Hotel. Another thing, dear, did you know you can get a jolly good free bath on Paddington Station? There's a very decent bathroom in the Great Western. You just go in there for a coffee and then trot upstairs to the ladies' room and along the corridor and you're in a very nice big bathroom with marble fittings and nice old brass chains to the plugs. Thundering hot water, dear. I take soap and a towel always when I'm in London. In a Harrods bag.'

'You could be arrested.'

'Rubbish. There's not a hint of a sign saying "Private". It says *Bathroom*. Nobody uses it but me because all the rooms are this ghastly thing *En Suite* now. Have you noticed on the motorway – the motels? "*24 En Suites*". I'd never stay in a place like the Great Western now, of course. It's only for commercial travellers. But the bathroom's useful if you have to change for the evening. It saves that nonsense of belonging to a so-called Club. Deadly places – all full of old women. Victoria Station was very good, too, before the War, and at St Pancras, The Great Northern, you could always stay a night no questions asked if you knew the ropes and wore the right clothes. They used to leave the keys standing in the doors. So unwise.

'And did you know you can spend *such* a pleasant hour or so in the London Library simply by ignoring the Members Only notice? You just walk in looking thoughtful and go upstairs to the Reading Room. It's a pity they've moved the old leather armchairs. They were so comfortable and you could sleep in them before a matinée. I always picked up one of the learned journals from the racks – something like *The John Evelyn Society Quarterly* – so that they'd think I was an old don.'

'They can see you're no don, Molly, with those diamonds.'

'I turn them round, dear. I'm not silly. They used to give you a tray of tea in the London Library once, you know, but all those nice things have stopped since the Conservatives got in. Look – an elastic band. It's the Post Office. I keep these. The postmen drop them all over England – all up the drive of the Final Resting Place. I told the postman they're worth money so now he drops them all through my letter box instead, great showers of them, like tagliatelle.'

We were walking on the common now. Lunch was over. It was a cold day and people were muffled up and pinched of face but Molly looked brisk and scarcely seventy. From the back – her behind neat, her legs and ankles skinny – she might have been forty-five. She wore a beautiful, old, lavender- mixture tweed suit and no glasses and she carried no stick. Trotting around her was a new puppy, a border collie she was training. She walked at a good speed through the spruces, as fast as I did and nearly as fast as the puppy, which she'd let off the lead. Her cheeks were pink, her eyes were bright and several people smiled at her as she went by. One old boy of about sixty gave her the eye and said he agreed about the wastage of elastic bands.

I said we should turn back as it was going to rain and she didn't want to be landed with a cold.

'I never catch cold,' she said. 'It's because I don't use public transport. I like my car. It was quite unnecessary for you to fetch and carry me today, you know. Very nice of you – but I'd have enjoyed crossing London again.'

'Do they let you drive still, Molly?' She had one of the little houses on an estate for the elderly she called the Final Resting Place.

'They can't stop me. Not yet. It's coming up of course – next driving test. Well, yes, they do fuss a bit. I can't remember where I'm going sometimes after I've set off, and the other day I couldn't remember where I'd been.'

'That might be a warning sign, you know, Molly. That it's time to stop.'

'Oh, fish! Wait till I get properly lost, then I'll stop. I've a card in my bag with my telephone number. I haven't forgotten who I am yet.'

'That does happen—'

'Oh, that Alzheimer business. That must be a terrible thing. But it only happens to the old, doesn't it?' She roared with laughter and clipped the dog on the lead.

Molly's dogs have always been wonderfully well-behaved and obedient – never smelled or chewed things or wet things or snapped or barked. Rather dispirited animals really. She never appeared to pay much attention to them. Years ago I remembered that she had said it was her mother who had taught her how to handle dogs.

'Come on,' she cried from the traffic island in the middle of the High Street. 'You'll get run over if you hang about. Make a dash.'

★

At tea – she'd done well at lunch with a couple of sherries and a glass of chablis with the chicken – she settled down to a crumpet and a long and interesting analysis of her investments. As usual I forgot altogether that Molly had been my grandmother's friend. I forgot the great string of years she had known, the winters and winters and winters, the spring after spring, flowing back and back and back to the first mornings of the century. I forgot the huge number of times she had woken to another day.

When I was a girl, Molly would come breezing by to see us in a fast car, usually with a woman friend, never with a man or her husband who had been, like her father, a shadow. (She had married in ten minutes, my grand-mother used to say, when her mother was upstairs in bed having measles of all things: absolutely furious, her mother was, too. In fact she died.) When I was a girl, I had always felt that Molly was empowered with an eternal youth, more formidable, much more effective, than my transient youth that seemed longer ago.

'Well, I'm not clever,' she often said. 'I'm a fool, dear. I know my limitations. No education and not a brain in my head. That's the secret. You're all so clever now – and all so good. It does age people. And also of course I'm frightfully mean. I don't eat or drink much unless I'm out.'

But she wasn't mean. When she gave a present, having said she could afford nothing, it tended to be stupendous. Once she gave me a car. And she did leave me one of the rings. But, 'I'm mean,' she said. 'And I'm not intellec-tual. I always wanted to be a racing driver after motor cars came in. Not allowed to, of course. D'you think I'm embittered?' (She shrieked with laughter.) 'I've struggled through. I've struggled through.'

And struggle it had sometimes looked to be – her freezing house, her empty hearth and fridge, her beautiful but ancient clothes all mended and pressed and hung in linen bags in the wardrobe. She had often sat wrapped in rugs to save coal. She had never had central heating. An ascetic pauper – until you looked at her investments, and they were wonderful. Whenever you saw her reading the financial columns she was smiling.

'*And*,' she said, 'hand it to me. I'm rational. That's what gets you through in the end, you know – being rational. I've no imagination, thank God. I give to charity but I've the sense not to watch the news. "Thank God" by the way is jargon. I don't believe in God and I don't believe that half the people I know who go to church and carry on at Christmas and go to the *Messiah* and that sort of thing – that they do either. All my Bridge lot, of course they don't believe in God. Religion's always seemed to me to be fairy stories. I go to church now and then, but it's for keeping up friendships and the look of it. And I quite enjoy weddings and funerals, of course.'

She was awesome, Molly. Awful really. But she was so nice.

She was in the midst of one of these 'I'm rational' conversations, the refrain that had threaded all my association with her, and she was eating her crumpet, and I was wondering why she was still insisting on her – well, on her boringness, and why she didn't bore me, why she never annoyed me; and I had decided it was because she never dissembled, that in my life her total truthfulness was unique. The truth Molly told showed her to be good. A good, straight being. Molly the unimaginative was unable to lie.

At which point she suddenly said, 'By the way, my mother's been seen around again.'

I looked at her.

'Around the village. And the FRP. She's looking for me, you know. But she won't find me.'

I said, 'Your *mother*?'

She said, 'Yes. You didn't know her. You were lucky. I hated her. Of course you know I did. You must have heard. She was very cruel to me. Well, she's back. Darling, are you going to take me home to the house of the near-dead? It's getting dark.'

'Yes, of course. Are you ready?'

'I'll just run upstairs.'

This she did and I waited with her coat and gloves and walking shoes and the basket with the dog's belongings and the dog.

'Yes,' she said coming down the stairs, twisting about at her knickers. 'Yes, she's been around for quite a time, a year or so. I don't know where she was before. I've managed to keep out of her way up to now. I hope that she didn't spot me leaving today, she'd have wanted to come, too.'

So, half an hour later I said, 'Molly, do you mean your *mother*?'

'Yes, dear. I'm afraid she was very unkind. I don't often talk about it. I was very frightened of her. D'you know, dear, I don't know when I've *had* such a wonderful day. Oh, how I've enjoyed it. Now if you turn left here and left again we can take the short cut and get straight to the bypass. You see I know exactly where I am. Now don't come in with me – you must get back before the traffic.'

I said, 'Molly—'

She kissed me, hesitated, and then got out. I saw her standing motionless before her mock-Georgian front door looking first at the lock, then at her key.

'Shall I open it?' I called to her.

'No, no. Of course not. Don't treat me as senile. Ninety-four is nothing. It won't be thought anything of soon. When you're ninety-four there'll be hundreds of you, with all this marvellous new medicine that's going on.'

'Goodbye, dear Molly. I'll wait till you're safe inside.'

'It's just that the lights aren't on.' She said, 'If you could just watch me in from the car. Just watch till I light everything up. It's so silly but I don't greatly like going into a dark house.'

I drove to the estate office and spoke to the lady superintendent who said that Molly was indeed still driving, though they were getting worried about it. She said that Molly was utterly sensible, utterly rational and her eyes and mind were very good. In fact she upset the younger ones by doing her stocks and shares and phoning her broker in the public common room.

'No aberrations? Does her mind wander?'

'*Never*,' she said. 'She is our star turn.'

★

Yet on the way home I decided to ring up her daughter, Alice, and was walking towards the phone the next morning when it began to ring, and it was Alice calling me. There were the statutory empty screams about how long since we'd spoken and then she asked if it were true that Molly had been to lunch with me. I said yes, and that I'd fetched her and taken her back, of course.

'Not 'of course' at all, ducky. Do you know she's still driving?'

I went on like the superintendent for a bit: about the beady eye that saw me look at the rings, the high-speed walk, the psychic hold over the dog, the fearlessness on the High Street, the splendid appetite. 'There was just—'

'Ha!'

'Well, she says her *mother* is about. Alice, her mother'd be about a hundred and thirty years old.'

'I know. Oh, heaven, don't I know. Did she say her mother's looking for her around the village?'

'Yes.'

'And making her clean her nails and polish her shoes and— She rings me up and asks me to bring a cake over because her mother's coming to tea. About twice a week.'

'But I've never heard her mention her mother before.'

'The doctors say it's the supply of oxygen to the brain. It's running uneven, like a car with dirty plugs. There are vacuums or something, and it's in the vacuums she really lives. Maybe it's where we all really live.'

'But all the bossy, sensible, happy years?'

'*All* the years. It was all there underneath, always. The fear.'

....

'Could we remind her of her mother's funeral? Would that end it?'

'She never went to the funeral. Her mother died abroad. I do say sometimes, "She's not here, Ma – she's dead and gone," but she just says, "I'm afraid not." She'll forget for a week and then remember. Then the terrors begin.'

'Whatever can the woman have done to her?'

Alice paused so long, that I thought we'd been cut off.

'Oh, I expect nothing much,' she said, in the end. 'Something quite hidden. It's just part of the horrors of old age.'

But at Molly's funeral I wasn't so sure. Among the extraordinarily large crowd – many of them young, many dog-lovers, some old, old racing-driver types, her solicitor, her stockbroker and a horde from the Final Resting Place, quite a few children – I could not rid myself of the notion that there was someone else present, just at my shoulder.

II: Signor Settimo

'There again,' they said in Spratpool Street. 'She's there again,' and they looked at each other and plodded on round the shops.

The horse lifted and dropped a hoof. The groom sat above on the polished seat of the trap. The trap was smarter than a carriage, quite chic and, like the County, expensive and correct but not yet a motor. It stood outside the studio of the new photographer and the groom stared ahead, knees stalwart under the rug, the Ironside groom, just about the last in Shipley.

Mrs Ironside was attending the photographer. All of sixty, squat as the old Queen, she was again attending the photographer, she was never away.

The first visit had been only a sighting from the road when the new studio was still an amazement in the town and she had directed the trap to pause there as she passed by, to allow her to examine the window.

A low, artistic signboard of bright wood was painted with gold lettering: 'Settimo. Portraiture', and behind it stood a huge, near life-size photograph of a newly married couple, the she in a mile of heavy lace, the he in half a bale of black, ill-fitting, foreign-looking suiting.

The she had her veil pulled down low over the brow with a little tight band of flowers, rather like a swimming cap. It gave her a glamorous ferocity. The sheaf of lilies across her lap lay like swords. The he stared hot-eyed, plump-cheeked, a broad silken moustache and tie, round-ended stiff collar, hair plastered flat on his head, gleaming; and on his ankles spats, grey spats above patent leathers. They were a serious, confident pair, not yet rich but determined. You could see the black ink of ledgers, the shouting and the passions, little leisure, and the children not having it easy. Mrs Ironside felt a liking for the two of them, almost recognition, though they clearly hadn't had much to do with Shipley.

Nothing at all to do with Shipley, for over their shoulders spread a crumbling hillside tremulous with laburnum, dark with chestnut trees, and roses showered over the tops of secret garden walls. A little donkey with panniers filled with grasses was being watched on its way by a peasant woman shading her eyes in a dusty, flowery lane. And all beneath a cloudless sky.

And this couple was seated upon an ornamental terrace before a marble balustrade and on the balustrade a slippery fringed shawl and on the shawl a flagon with an inviting lip and beside the flagon a great glass jar with a carved glass stopper. The jar seemed stuffed with spiral layers of orchard fruits, strange, syrupy, glowing things catching the light.

The photograph had already created a stir in Shipley. Often little groups had gathered on the pavement in the cold spring winds and steady northern English rain saying, Look at them pears and plums, you could sink your teeth in them, queer aren't they, you can see right through to the gowks. You can just feel the silk in that shawl. He'll be expensive I dare say. It'll be for carriage folk I dare say.'

Florrie Ironside was carriage folk nowadays all right and had been for a long time. Expense meant nothing to her in her jet necklaces and black ruched satin and first-quality Shipley woollen pelisse, her beaded hat from Harrogate, her chunks of ugly jewellery and the vast brass-framed cameo attached to her bosom. The cameo held a tinted representation of her dead husband and a twist of his sandy hair. Florence Ironside sat under a black umbrella in the rain and examined the new shop-front painted coffee-cream with lighter cream blinds each with a golden tassel. It stood between Bogey's Grocers full of cheeses stuck with gluey linen, and Batty's Drapers (founded 1812) stacked up with bales of wool and tweeds and calicos, and fans of cards of button hooks and linen-covered singlet-buttons. Outside the new shop a young man in thin shoes was locking the door behind him as he went off to his lunch. His coat didn't look the cloth for a Shipley spring.

'A newcomer,' she said to the groom, who said he'd heard tell a Hitalian.

A while later Florrie Ironside saw the young man again changing the window, and she stopped the trap to watch. He was lifting away the happy Italian couple and replacing them with a bride alone, startlingly dark, her hair falling in polished ripples, a great Nottingham veil dragging down behind her and swinging round into a pool at her feet. The dress had a straining satin bodice with no shame. The mouth was soft and sulky, swollen with desire; and, good gracious heaven, was the mouth of Hilda Staples' sullen Nellie! Who could have made a beauty of that slow lump? And sitting before that transfer screen with all the moral messages on it and the improving pictures – there was Mr Gladstone with his rose – the sort of thing decent children used to stick together with flour paste to fill up a winter. If it was Nellie, no wonder the bodice was tight, and just as well that bouquet was the size of a haystack. She looked sultry, though. She'd be admired.

Two sets of fingertips set Nellie gently on the easel and, over the top of her, Signor Settimo's sad eyes met the eyes of Mrs Ironside in the trap. As the photographer moved sideways and forwards for a moment, to look Nellie over, she saw that he seemed now rather better dressed. He was a delicate-looking young man with a pale face and dark hair pomaded down, the body slight as if it had taken no account of itself since it belonged to a stripling – shoulders birdlike, sloped hips and waist like a dancer's. All this – as he turned and looked at Mrs Ironside again – with a sense of yearning, of honey for sale. He vanished behind the bead curtain.

I might get the dog done, said Mrs Ironside, and then aloud, 'I might get the dog done. I've never had the dog done,' and the groom cocked an ear to see if he was to turn and go to the veterinarian's in the High Street. But no command came.

A few days later the trap was again outside the studio and

Mrs Ironside handing the dog down to the groom, who carried it in. Mrs Ironside sat stately and waiting, and time passed. Mrs Ironside even had to haul on the reins now and then to keep the pony steady, something she was perfectly able to do even in her black stuff costume, having been a farmer's daughter and well known, before she married Ironside who had made her so rich, for bumping down into Shipley in a shabby old habit on a shabby old cob every Thursday market day.

The groom emerged nervous. There had to be appointments. Yes, he'd said that. Yes, he'd tried – that's why he had been all this time – and, yes, even for dogs. And dogs was altogether dubious anyway. This Settims didn't care for dogs. This Settims stood his distance and got out his handkerchief, sneezing, having some nose trouble. He often drew the line at dogs.

Florrie Ironside then flung the reins away and crashed into the studio with the dog hanging down front and back under her arm. The groom stood waiting, and soon watching the arrival and angry departure of a mother with her swansdowned child. The woman recognised the Ironside conveyance and told the groom that her appointment had been cancelled for a dog, and she might even say for a bitch. The groom, who knew when he was well off (for jobs were scarce), looked steadily ahead and did not reply.

Mrs Ironside was with Signor Settimo a good three-quarters of an hour and emerged flushed with success, and the dog hanging limp even for a dachshund. Over luncheon with her daughter, Molly, she described the triumphant morning. It had been a struggle to get the better of this Italian even though he was so quiet. He had just stood there at first, watching her and smiling and apologising in a slimy sort of way. He hadn't given an inch until she had told him where she stood in the town, and Mr Ironside's position there, though dead. And that her address was The Mount. Then he'd been decisive and sensibly got on with the job. Not very talkative, though. Well, he'd certainly learned that foreigners in Shipley have to stand back.

Molly said she'd heard that he was a very *good* photographer and Mrs Ironside had said, Well, we shall see; and that he was taking a very long time to produce any proofs of his photographs. *Three weeks*, if you please, *three weeks*! 'Pressure of work' – and not able to get away to deliver even in the lunch-hours now, if you please. If you asked her it was all show and lies.

On the day promised for the delivery of the proofs of the portrait of the dog, Mrs Ironside arranged herself and Molly around the silver tea service in the drawing room at four o'clock as usual and as usual proceeded to eat up all the tea. Signor Settimo was to call at a quarter to five, and an upright chair had been placed for him at an appropriate distance. Mrs Ironside was for the first time since her widowhood wearing colour – a bunch of cloth violets against the black foulard of her dress above poor old Willy's good-natured face and wisp of dead hair. Molly across on the humpty was also looking neither one thing nor the other, for her mother in a fit of boredom had said Yes, she might bob her hair, and then in a fit of pique, No, she might not shorten her skirts.

So, ridiculous in flounces below her neat modern little head, Molly sat sideways reading a motoring monthly in which lean girls with flying scarves and cigarette holders clasped in their teeth lay back at the wheels of long chassis and sped across the pages like the wind. Their proud, painted, selfish faces stirred Molly. They rattled her. She said, 'I'm glad about the violets, Ma. It's well over the year. Well over. Black, black – it doesn't suit me and Pa wouldn't care.'

Her mother stared as if the fireguard had spoken. She said, 'Your father liked me in black. Black gives authority.'

'Well, I'd like a sea-green now. I'd like one of those motoring duster-coats and actually a car.' (And a man, she thought, to get me away. Any man. I wonder what the Eyetie's like? She's not used to men. She'll shred him. Poor old Pa with his belly and his sandy hair.)

A bell rang faintly far away and Mrs Ironside instructed Molly to eat the last piece of bread and butter. Molly asked if she should order fresh tea but her mother said no, and a maid came in with a package.

'Where is Mr Settimo?'

'He said, mum, he couldn't wait, mum.'

'Couldn't?'

'Said he couldn't, mum, pressure of work, mum. Sends his compliments and the bill for the proofs is in the separate envelope.'

Mrs Ironside thrust up her chin and turned a little blue about the lips and breathed slowly. She slapped down her crumby plate and said, 'Take the tea things. Give me the package. Why isn't it on a salver? What! Account! This isn't an account, it is a ransom. It's more than a doctor!'

But inside the package was a sleek and knowing hound, each hair gleaming, jokey frown-lines wrinkling between the eyes as if he were the most intelligent animal of the ark, as if he were perhaps even trying to understand Italian. His paddle feet hung down showing his beautifully manicured nails and his ears were lifted charmingly and alertly at the root.

'Oh, Ma! It's wonderful! He's the most *wonderful* photographer!'

Mrs Ironside sat all evening in her chair lifting the proofs of the dog one by one, holding them close to her eyes and then at arm's length. She returned them next day via the groom marked up for enlargement and a note in her wild green ink saying that the account would be settled in full the following week when her considerable order was completed. She gave instructions to the maids that when Mr Settimo called he was to be shown round to the back door.

But he did not come. Not to either door. Not the next week, nor the one after, nor the one after that. And at last when the groom was sent down to the studio he found a notice in the window saying, *Temporarily closed owing to family bereavement in Cremona*, and Nellie Staples displaced for a swathe of crepe.

'Unprofessional,' said Florrie Ironside. 'Unnecessary. And what has Cremona got to do with it? I thought it was toffee. He'll get nowhere if he can't stick to his last. I'm sure *we* could never afford to go running about overseas when your father was making his way.'

Molly (eighteen) said, 'But he's young, Ma,

you know, and he hasn't any ties. He's only about twenty.'

'Forty-five if a day,' said Florrie, fuming. 'Foreigners are deceptive. All talk and guile. You should remember what your father used to say about them after we'd been to Dusseldorf for our silver wedding. No – he'll go bankrupt.'

But later the next day the photographs of the dog were delivered directly to the back door by Signor Settimo's personal messenger dressed in coffee-coloured uniform and pill-box hat and white gloves under the epaulette. Mind you, May, the maid, said ask her and she'd say it was George Bickerstaffe's Henry with his face washed and the suit come from that overgrown page at the Regal cinema.

Mrs Ironside said only, 'Messenger, my eye,' and sent for the trap and directed it to Spratpool Street.

In they swept.

'Mr Settimo,' demanded Florence of the girl at the desk, who was in coffee-coloured sateen and jewelled bandeau, writing slowly in an order book with her tongue out.

'He's engaged.'

'*Engaged*!'

'He's with a sitter. I can't get at him. Not when he's under the cloth.'

'Produce him at once. I am Mrs Ironside.'

The girl knew this. She was Netta Cricklewood of Bogey's Grocers before being a Shipley solicitor's tea-girl and she had known Mrs Ironside from childhood.

She sidled off ('Half an inch of paint and silk stockings') and returned looking sulky with fear.

'He says to sit down and take a browse through the albums.'

There was one spindly gold chair, which Florrie regarded with venom while Mollie, who had been brought along, stood at the glass door looking out, hoping for motors.

'Come away from there,' said Florrie, 'D'you want all Shipley to know we're being kept waiting by a tradesman?' and she glared at Netta Cricklewood and asked if she wasn't missing her earlier professional career.

Netta — could it be her portrait above the desk, a sea nymph all bare skin and lip-gloss like a concubine? — Netta, recovering, said, 'Thank you very much, I'm not missing anything at all these days.'

At last came Settimo, clashing through the bead curtain and bowing out the sitter — an excited shadow — and turning to Mrs Ironside his gentle and impervious face.

He bowed.

'I have brought my account.'

'How very prompt. I am greatly obliged.'

'The photographs were very late.'

'I was called away to Cremona.' He let his eyes drift over her black, and old Willy smiling away on her chest. 'In Italy we also pay attention to mourning.'

Molly waited for her mother to embark on the sermon about the necessity for the bereaved to allow hard work to deal with grief and how she herself had *immediately* taken up the reins, winding up a great business with no assistance from anyone, except an only child who knew nothing, not even how to deal with the letters of condolence.

Instead she heard her mother ask if he would photograph her daughter. She, Molly.

Signor Settimo, not wavering by a flicker in Molly's direction, brushed Netta aside and negotiated the appointment himself in the leather-bound book.

Going home, Molly said, 'But I don't want my photograph taking, Ma. Why should I be photographed? I'm not a baby or a bride. They'll think you're trying to get me off.'

'Nonsense. I want a photograph of you for the drawing room. It's always wise to have a likeness. You never know what's going to happen. Look at the Duke of Clarence.'

Molly then wondered if she was going to die and her mother knew something she didn't. She went up and peered in the glass and decided she looked tubercular and became so taken with the idea that she considered making her will until she remembered that she had no money. She sat looking at her mother that evening, trying to see her sitting there soon alone, and maybe weeping. But Molly had a poor imagination.

When the photographs came, Mrs Ironside put them aside with scarcely a glance. 'I'm afraid you haven't your mother's presence, Molly.' Molly, flat-chested, taut, anonymous, sat bemused.

For there had been something very queer about Signor Settimo at the sitting, tip-tapping about the studio floor as if he was in church, arranging the folds of the cloth on a trellis behind her – nearer and nearer, circling nearer, touching her cheekbone at last; directing her head to look now at the Pantheon, now at the Bridge of Sighs and now – just here over his head – at the Campanile at Cremona. His neat little shanks made a pair of back legs for the angular dragonfly that fixed its great eye on her.

Molly was unnerved. Again and yet again she waited tensely for him to slide beneath the pall that was the creature's back, to crash the great brass plates together, then to plunge under again and call out his muffled directions. Out would dangle an arm holding in its fingers a soft grey rubber bulb on the end of a tube – there'd been something terrible and exactly like it the nurse used to bring when her father was dying – and the fingers would give a sudden expert squeeze and the flash of deadly lightning would strike.

'These will be very excellent photographs,' said Signor Settimo.

'Will they be as good as the dog's?'

He came dancing across to her then, and lifted dove-like hands on either side of her face as if to cup it. Then he stopped and let the hands and his head tip together first one way then the other as he smiled with the whitest of teeth and the most affectionate lips. He then appeared to recollect himself, and Molly unexpectedly thought of the groom who muttered, 'Jobs is scarce.'

'Miss Ironside,' said Signor Settimo, 'Signorina Ironside – I should very much like to photograph your mother.'

★

'He said he wanted to photograph you,' said Molly. They were riding lugubriously up and down Shipley leaving cards on people on a dank and sunless afternoon.

'Insolence,' said Florrie, and then, 'Well, I dare say he does. I'm not surprised. The prices he charges he'll need a good bit of advertisement.'

'He's put me in the window.'

'What? He hasn't dared! Without permission? For everyone to see? We have been good enough to give him trade and he hasn't asked permission? How dare he! We're going there at once.' And she gave the groom a prod in the back and they turned about.

In the window of Spratpool Street, there sat straight-eyed Molly with her frozen shoulders awaiting the lightning, and beside her, Lily, daughter of Alderman Bellinger, the late Mr Ironside's most vulgar and thrusting competitor in the building trade, who had posthumously absorbed him though at an exorbitant price. Lily's portrait was bigger than Molly's.

'This must be stopped. Wait here.' And Florrie was into the shop in three strides. And very quickly out of it again.

Signor Settimo was now on holiday. 'At The Grand at Scarborough,' said Netta with awe. There was only her there, and the messenger. The messenger was sitting looking rather ill on the ornamental chair, picking his teeth. He was without his pill-box and didn't get up.

'I shall complain in writing. Take my daughter from the window.'

'I'd never dare.'

'Then you—' She pointed. She grabbed the messenger by the neck.

161

'I've not got to touch things,' he said. 'I've got unnatural damp hands.'

'Then I shall.'

And Molly (and Shipley) saw the black arm of Mrs Ironside appear like King Arthur's in reverse and pluck her from the window.

Mrs Ironside was considerably upset and didn't speak all the way home or during tea. She sat in heavy thunder all the evening and the next day when Molly, frightened, at last said, 'There's no need to mind, you know, Ma. He can't hurt you. I mean, you're an old woman and he's only a boy.'

Then Mrs Ironside leaned across the breakfast table and slapped Molly across the face.

'She did,' said May, who'd been at the sideboard replenishing one of the big steel domes with bacon. 'She did. She slapped her face! And there's Molly runs out and up the stairs crying. That's the front door. Run and get it. I'm hot and cold all over.'

The bell had been rung by Signor Settimo hastening early from the studio in his new motor to apologise for the bish about Molly and Lily Bellinger. The breakfast room door was still open and Mrs Ironside was shaking at the table, shocked and prior to weeping, but the weeping she set aside. She found her heart was beating fast. She ordered the maid to show the photographer into the morning room. Breathing slowly now, she sat on for a little, wondering at the wonderful sense of lightness in her, the triumph within. She went out to him.

Settimo stood in the window of the morning room beside the metal storks. He stood upon a rich Turkey rug admiring the polish on all the mahogany, the shine on the Dutch tiled grate, the bloom on the escritoire. His fingers stroked a Chinese pot on a plinth of inlaid walnut. Above his head hung the very latest thing – a metal drum with a pink silk frill that contained bulbs of electricity. It was like looking up skirts.

'Cremona,' he was saying, 'Oh, Cremona!'

'Mrs Ironside,' he said, 'how I should like to make a commemorative album of this house! How nearly it is like my home.'

'Cremona?' Florrie was feeling lighter and lighter; a victor, yet joyously damned. 'Cremona?'

He told her about Northern Italy, the watery flatness of the plains, the reedy River Po (which he pronounced as in pot or tot or clot, in the best possible taste), the dark canyons of the old streets of its cities and how, in Cremona, his own city, the narrow toppling alleys flung black flags of shade. He told how you burst out from under them into the bright sunlight of the piazzas, light that softly bathed the street-long baroque palaces, the gold and pale-pink churches, the tightly bound but generously bulging, beckoning cathedral. He described the boom of the bells, the jingle of the little carriages all ribbons and plumes, the café tables shining with thick linen cloths under the pillars round the cathedral square. There you could sit talking, talking long into the summer night, and nobody to hurry you away.

'Cremona is the essence of dignity and culture and civilisation. Keep Firenze. Keep Roma.'

'I wonder that you could bear to leave it, Mr Settimo.'

'I wonder, too, but in Cremona there are many photographers. All is weddings – weddings and weddings. Weddings and babies. I was so seldom called upon to photograph a face of experience, of knowledge of the world.'

Florence Ironside was booked in for a sitting at 2.30 p.m. the following Tuesday.

But it was not a success.

Signor Settimo was desolate. It was not a success. Florence (prophetic name) was not herself – hush! He meant it. 'This is not yourself, not your real self sitting there. You pretend to be so bold, so, if you will forgive me, so tight drawn-up. But I cannot see *you*. I cannot feel your essence. All I see and feel are your – certainly magnificent – strength and your ferocity. Hush, yes, your ferocity. Your *enmity*. Oh, relax please, Signora Ironside, you electrify the air.'

'I don't know what you're talking about,' said Florence, lifting her chin, confronting the dragonfly optic and the black hump of Settimo laid along behind. She felt excited. He thought he'd catch her, did he, with all that about sunshine and piazzas? Little Signor Settimo and she, the widow of Willy Ironside of Shipley. She curled her rather pretty, scornful little lips. There came the squeeze and the flash and the crash of thunderbolts and he took the photograph that a long time later went the rounds.

It is always the wrong photograph that goes the rounds.

He came over and stood looking down into her face and said, 'Signora – why are you belligerent?'

'Your English is very good,' she said.

'Of course. I am from Cremona. Do you think I am a Sardinian? Or educated in Shipley?'

He made her sit in the hard spotlight and slid back under the cloth. The silence returned. The bulb was held high, but was not pressed.

Mrs Ironside's face changed, the small eyes widened, the chin sank down. The lips seemed to soften. He came over and directed the cheekbone towards the Bridge of Sighs. He touched the shoulder of the armoured dress. He lifted one of the hands across the breast, screening poor old Willy.

'I'll take this off,' said Florence, unpinning the brooch, wondering if she had been told to do so or if it was her own idea.

Under the pall he cried, 'Oh – that is so much better. But still – no, I still do not see you. You are unpractised. You cannot give. There is something withheld, something secret about you. Am I looking at a woman or a cold machine? A frightened – forgive me – old maid?'

He squeezed the bulb listlessly and the lightning seemed scarcely to flicker.

'There will be no charge,' he said. 'You have not trusted me. You cannot give. You shall return next week.' He walked with her only as far as the door of the darkroom and dismissed her inattentively.

'He said he wouldn't charge me,' she said to Molly, who had asked no questions and now said nothing. 'And I should think not. He was entirely at fault. He was out of sorts. Very temperamental.' She thought of the horrible slapping of Molly's face. 'Well, who isn't, from time to time. Especially after bereavement. I'm afraid I am sometimes temperamental myself. I do thoughtless things sometimes. I'm sorry, Molly.'

Molly, amazed, said, 'I don't think *I* am temperamental.'

'Oh, but you see all Italians are, and you have your father's colouring, Scottish colouring. I wonder if I have a little drop of Italian blood.'

'They say he's overspending,' said Molly. 'May says there are bills as long as your arm everywhere. And that car isn't paid for, May says. He's in trouble.'

'Oh, but I think he's been used to wealth. He tells me that in Cremona there are streets of nothing but palaces. He only travels for his Art.'

'Are you going back to him then? I know I wouldn't. Ma – I was a bit afraid of him.'

'Oh, of course I'm going back. I'm not a churlish woman, I hope.'

For the next sitting she left off the mourning brooch, laying it down on her dressing table, and turned back into her bedroom at the last minute to change her hat for a great Leghorn straw swooning with flat roses – cream roses – and a veil that tied under the chin, this time with a white velvet ribbon.

'Ah—' said Settimo. 'There! Exactly. Yes. Just like that. Lift the chin a fraction – do not pretend to be *demure*. It hasn't come to that. Smile at me. Mrs Ironside, I have never seen you openly smile. But that is beautiful. Oh, how beautiful – your lovely smile. You have the lips of a young madonna, Mrs Ironside. Delicious under the veil.'

His pointed fingers were on her shoulder as she left. 'But, I want more.' He was like a sympathetic doctor. They were alone. Netta and the messenger were nowhere to be seen. She suddenly remembered for some reason that little Henry Bickerstaffe had measles and that Wednesday anyway was Shipley's early-closing day.

He moved his fingers across the back of her neck to the knot of ribbon that held the veil. 'I should like to undo this veil. I should like to see – perhaps unpin – your hair. Had I the money – any money, I am over-spent. I am in deep, deep water owing to circumstances in Cremona – had I any money, I would dress you as a Princess of Piedmont. I would drop your awful English jewels in the river and I would adorn you with moonstones.'

He sent for her again the following Wednesday and she went to him on foot and ('I'm not imagining this, I saw it from the end of Blenheim Terrace and Mrs Cricklewood saw it, too') she went hatless. Perhaps gloveless. He held back the bead curtain, first drawing down the blind that said 'Half Day Wednesday' over the glass front door. She passed before him into the darkroom.

'All right then. Tek me to Scarborough. I'll say nothing if you'll tek me to Scarborough. Mind you, half Shipley knows. They're all asking me.'

'Netta, I can't take anyone anywhere. This is the reason about the abeyance of the wages. I am in trouble. I am an artist – you know that – not a businessman. I need a business partner of character, if possible with great capital. That is all there is to say. I take you into my confidence. I never have trouble in finding business partners. Never. I have every hope of money – even for Scarborough – quite soon.'

'You mean my Auntie Florrie?'

'Auntie?'

'It's not a real auntie. "Auntie" 's what you call your mother's best friends in England. You may not have it in Cremona. Auntie Florrie was at school with my mam. Auntie Florrie had to walk in to Shipley school five miles. Her Molly and me, we went to different schools, Molly's being private, but *she* was always my Auntie Florrie. She married rich and you see what's become of her, sitting up at that great place and Molly like a cold drink of water and neither of them with a thing to do. Tek me to The Grand. You're on the wrong tack up there, Ferdinando.'

'I don't know what you mean.'

'Half Shipley does then. It's the wonder of the world. And those that knows laughs their heads off and thinks you're a daftie.'

'A – what?'

'I don't know it in Italian. Will you tek me to Scarborough?'

'I can *not*.'

'Then I'll tell yer. I know where you went to the so-called funeral. It was your engagement party – I opened the photos. And I'll tell you you're up the wrong tree with Auntie Florrie. She hasn't a penny after Molly's thirty-five. It's all going to be Molly's. I saw it in the will when I was being a solicitor.'

Signor Settimo looked steadily at Netta with his clever eyes angry and little like those of the Piedmontese bridegroom. He then left her and stepped into his car.

He roared out of Spratpool Street and hurtled out of the town, way past Ilkley and on to the purple moors. Hours went by and in the end the car seemed to drift and sway, to turn back and to take itself home via the dachas on the green slopes surrounding Shipley.

Molly, the girl so mad about cars, Molly, so innocent, so eager for life. Oh, the mistake he had made. He cursed himself. He had an insane desire to proceed at once to The Mount, to sweep up the deep trenched gravel of its drive, to ask to see Molly. But, impossible now.

Yet as he drew near, at the end of The Mount's driveway he let the car dawdle and stop and after a time he heard footsteps crunching in the gravel and he got out of the car and took off his tight little driving helmet and waited.

But it was only the groom in a muffler and an old coat trailing the dog along behind him; and the groom gave him a look of pity as he passed.

Then the groom called back over his shoulder as he went off down the hill, 'Whichever you're after you're out of luck, Maestro. They're gone, the pair of them. They're gone touring off foreign and both of them miserable, thanks to you. You've ruined them with your magic lanterns.'

III: The Hot Sweets of Cremona

Molly Fielding's daughter Alice and the woman Molly Fielding had liked and had left a ring to were sitting together drinking under the stone canopy and inside the forest of pillars of the great piazza of Cremona. It was a month or so after old Molly's funeral.

They had been a little nervous of going on holiday together. It had been rashly, emotionally arranged, the ghost of the old woman the only bond, for as girls they had not got on, Alice too vehement and self-conscious for the other one.

And their lives and marriages had been very different. The friend was a reticent widow whom Alice had always found rather dull, and Alice was a recent divorcee whom the friend had always thought shallow and too talkative. They were relieved now to find that their conventional upbringing was helping them through the blind spots and the dark pools, that they knew the antique rules for Englishwomen of a certain age on holiday abroad. 'Mustn't forget the postcards. God, so expensive!' 'How about doing our sums? You did these drinks. I paid for the tummy medicine' – and so on. They had looked up assiduously the opening and closing times of the galleries, underlining everything marked with two or three stars.

Alcohol had helped as it does after funerals. They were drinking vermouth now out of little gold-rimmed glasses shaped like convolvus flowers and thinking contentedly that it would soon be lunchtime when there would be wine. After a long siesta they would then set off and wander in the cathedral again, maybe take a little carriage and jingle round the streets of the city. And then – my dear, a *divine* dinner in the dark hotel with the dazzling white cloths thick as blankets, and those great jars of crystallised fruits gleaming on the central table. 'Like Mantegnas,' said the rather educated friend, and Alice said, 'And we'll try the fegato.'

They sighed and leaned back gazing at the piazza; sixtyish, well-heeled, well-dressed and pleased not to be young.

'I'm pleased not to be young.' The friend examined old Molly's ring on her finger.

'Italy tore me to bits, you know, when I was young,' said Alice.

'All that passion. God – how did we survive? How did we get anything else *done*? Why does time go by so much faster now that we've nothing to do – nothing to obsess us? D'you realise, nobody will ever kiss us any more.'

The other one looked across the sunny square criss-crossed by Romeos and Juliets on glittering scooters. The girls tossed their hair and clasped their hands round the boys' waists, rested their beautiful faces sideways against the boys' warm leather backs. Frighteningly positive, they didn't look as if they dawdled over kissing.

The friend knew, and so did Alice, that she had meant to say fuck not kiss, but it had not been possible. They were too old to be able to say aloud the once unthinkable word without seeming outrageous or pathetic, just as they could not wear a skirt halfway up the thigh.

It was not characteristic, rather drunk-sounding, for Alice to say next, 'You can tell when women have stopped being kissed, it's when the lips go indistinct round the edges and the lipstick goes jammy. That was one of Ma's little adages: "Over fifty and lipstick goes jammy." '

'I fell in love with a German in Florence my first time in Italy,' said the friend, 'when I was eighteen. Just after the war. He looked wonderful, like Galahad. I was confused. We'd all just seen the Belsen films. He was so gentle.'

'I came to Italy as an au pair about then,' said Alice, 'to a grand Roman family. Their last au pair had died in a bath at the other end of the Palazzo and they hadn't found her for three days. They thought it was *funny*! So poor! They were so poor there was only pasta. I did learn how to eat it though, not to wind it round the fork like the servants did, or so I was told. Some foreign royalty came once and the daughter really did take down curtains to make a dress. Eighteenth-century ones. All dust in the folds. It was a wonderful dress, too. The Conte made the usual passes. No, he wasn't the one. It was the gardener. Under the olives. On the Campagna. Marvellous. Ma came out to get me back when I wouldn't come home. Thank God, I suppose. Well – I *suppose*. She dragged me off to Parma to buy a

ham on the way back! "So cheap, dear." A great purple
shank of it. And me weeping.'

'Molly could be pretty ruthless. I saw a photo of her
mother once, your grandmother. I suppose that's where
it came from.'

'Oh, no,' said Alice. 'No, no, not from her mother.
Not from Granny Ironside. Granny put up a good act but
she wasn't ruthless in the least.'

'But you never could have met her, Alice. She died
before your mother married. How do you know she
wasn't ruthless?'

'Mother told me. In a way.'

'But she told me, Molly told *me*, not long ago, the day
she came to lunch last winter and ran about the common,
Molly told me that she'd been very frightened of her
mother. Said she was a cruel and terrible woman. Well,
but you and I talked about it. Awful.'

'Oh, Granny Ironside frightened her all right. Granny
Ironside wasn't exactly maternal. But she wasn't ruthless. It was Molly, my ma, who was the ruthless one.
Pitiless to herself, too. Ma dealt with her passions like a
nun. She seemed – well, she was – affectionate later on,
but, you know, amusing, charming Ma was really cold as
a fish. She was totally unintuitive and she hadn't a clue
about her mother. Her mother needed a mighty rescue.'

'You mean from – where was it – Wigan?'

'Shipley. No. Not a rescue from Shipley. Granny
Ironside needed a rescue from her awful fate, her awful,
sealed–off, uneducated, empty life. She was a more
significant woman than Ma. She went a bit mad, you
know. A lot of those women did. That photo of her is a

bit mad when you look at it. Dangerously pent-up. She's supposed to have fallen in love with someone absolutely impossible after Grandpa Ironside died. Ma never said who, but she knew. Something to do with a measles epidemic, so maybe it was a doctor. No, I mean it. God knows who he was, it's all garbled. Look, Granny was ugly and sixty and over-rich and the only man she'd ever known was a Shipley builder who left the town only once to go on a builders' spree to Dusseldorf and was out every night of the week in a Shipley pub drinking with his men. She had one child – Ma. Ma, who liked only fast cars, and was cold and bored. Poor Granny – no lover. *Nobody* loved her. Nobody really liked her much. She didn't know how to be likable. And she'd grown far too rich for her country childhood friends.'

'But there was a lover? You said so.'

'I said she fell in love. She was being manipulated in some way, so the story goes. Ma knew it all but she pretended to forget. What she did say was that Granny and nobody else except the solicitor knew that Grandpa had left all the money to her, to Molly, when she was thirty-five. Do you know, it's the cruellest thing a man can do, a will like that? No, maybe it's crueller not to tell the wife and let her find out. Granny did know. All Grandpa Ironside left her was his tinted photograph to wear as a brooch. She wore it, too. And full mourning for a year. D'you think she was hoping for pity when Ma came into the money? The lover I suppose must just have faded out.'

'But wasn't she a dragon? I can see that Settimo photograph now. The first and famous Settimo.

My mother had a copy. Settimos are collectors' pieces now.'

'That was the only way she knew how to look. She'd never had a touch of tenderness. D'you know how Granny Ironside died? Do you know what happened?'

'Well – nobody knew. That's what I heard. It was here in Italy. In Cremona. Something not good about it. Didn't Molly somehow miss the funeral? Some scandal?'

'*I* know. I know Ma's version anyway. I got the hang of it through Ma's craziness at the end. I know why she was scared of Grandma's ghost. The ghost that lay in wait.'

'But what had she *done* to Molly?'

'She took her off. Made her leave Shipley. A matter of hours after she realised the lover wanted only Ma's money. She rushed Ma out of England. All Shipley laughing.'

'At Molly?'

'No. At her. At poor old Florrie. She'd been conned by the mysterious lover and they all knew. She, iron Mrs Ironside of The Mount. She'd been wild for him the last weeks. Hung about outside his house, followed him in the street, showered him with presents. Then she must have found Ma was after him too, or he was after Ma when he somehow found out about the money. She wasn't going to leave Ma behind for him, so she swept her off to Italy. Ma (can you believe it?) caught measles. I haven't found out all about these measles or where they came from but there was *something*. Ma had measles not badly but badly enough and when they'd reached Milan and she was getting better she used to sit forlorn in the hotel while Granny went violently about seeing the sights. There's a Last Supper or something. Well, in the hotel there was a middle-aged Englishman in a nice checked suit. He had sandy hair like Ma's father. He was the only man Ma had ever been in a room alone with and he was as bored as she was with Italy and they talked about cars. He drove a Lagonda and lived near Epsom. Perfect for her, my old Pa. They were engaged in five days.

'She never said a word of course. Granny hurtled her off to Florence and Siena, and bashed her round galleries, churches, the lot, beating down her own humiliation, wild as a fury till Ma was tired out and said, "No more. I want to go home."

'They had reached here, Cremona. Granny had got stranger than ever. She was tramping the city alone at night. She would come back at midnight and fling herself across a bed. Whaleboned, stout Victorian matron, taught that you never go out unchaperoned and never show your love.

'The evening Ma broke down and said she was going to get married to the man in the checked suit they were in the hotel dining room. It might even have been our hotel. It probably was. It's still the only good one. Granny took a great bottle of those fruit things and flung it to the ground and smashed it. And she took hold of Ma round the neck and shook and shook her. Yes. The management had to separate them and put Granny Ironside to bed. Can you imagine! "*Inglese! Non possibile!*" etc. And off goes Ma on the train the same night, all alone, to Milan and the founder member of the Lagonda Club. My father-to-be.'

'But whatever—?'

'Whatever happened to Florence Ironside? She caught the measles and died. She "had them on her", as they say. She caught them badly and her heart gave way. She's buried here – well, you know that, I told you. My poor old grandmamma. Daddy came from Milan and saw to it all. Consul, telegrams, funeral. Ma told me that he thought she should have come back here with him, but she sat it out in Milan. That's why she wasn't at her mother's funeral.

'I didn't know till Ma's end, her terrible end when her mother's presence was eating away under the surface of the memory – the awful last bit, when Florrie stood about the streets and lanes of Rickmansworth watching for her daughter, in the corners of rooms or peeping from windows or just inside the front door of her little house at the Final Resting Place. But it was then, when Ma had begun to plead with me to buy her dead mother sponge cakes for tea, that I began to think about Grandma.'

'Not to start *liking* her?'

'Understanding her. A little. I know now that what she was saying to Ma in the Last Battle of Cremona, throwing the fruit about, was that Ma should marry only for love. It wouldn't matter if the man did not love her. Forget that. If she never out-and-out loved someone (and you know Ma never did; not out-and-out; certainly not me; certainly not Pa, she didn't bother with him much even when he was dying, she was at a car rally), if her daughter was never going to *love* someone, love till it aches, said Granny Ironside, she'd be dead for ever. To

marry for escape, to marry for money, to marry from
boredom, or for protection or security were immoral
motives. Granny Ironside was ahead of her time. She had
come to see – God knows how – that Victorian, middle-
class marriage was most terribly sad.

' "And *disgusting*," apparently she roared at Ma, at
Molly her taut little daughter. (And think: sex was never
mentioned then between mother and daughter except in
a creepy whispering way.) "You'll lie there in the bed
every night putting up with it, going through with it,
maybe in the end not altogether disliking it, even in a
vague way looking forward to it, at last treating it like a
ridiculous duty. Immoral! Pathetic! Oh, you antiseptic,
grasping girls." "For God's sake, *love*," she was crying,
and all the Piedmontese as shocked as an English
boarding house as they dragged her up the stairs. All so
sorry for Molly sitting there clutching her dinner napkin.
Such a bleak little face.

'So Ma left Cremona an hour later. Left her mother the
bill, and it was vast because of the broken fruits, and sent
Daddy to clear up.'

'But Molly did love people, Alice. She loved lots of
people. Look at the huge funeral.'

'She was *affectionate* – as affectionate and nice as pie.
But I don't think Daddy had much of a time. It was
separate rooms from the start, you know, and you never
saw a cooler widow. I'm very much an only child. After
Pa, it was always women friends. No more men. *And* she
was always bringing them to Italy. No reverberations.
Just charming, leisurely little motoring tours. God – how
could she? Lipstick, permed hair, good clothes and

everything treated lightly. She kept clear of thinking. No religion, no politics (except you couldn't even *know* a socialist), no failures, no pain. Not a weed in her garden. Her table silver always shining, and a garage like an operating theatre, not a spot of oil on the floor. Love? Not a breath of it, ever.'

'She did mock, rather.'

'Oh, she mocked me about loving Italy. She came here, it always seemed to me, to cock a snook at it. "You never caught me, see!" But she used to say to me, "You're being Italian again, Alice, with your big black eyes. I wonder where you came from? If you'd been Granny's daughter not mine we wouldn't have been surprised." '

'It sounds as if Florrie's lover was *Italian*.'

'The only Italians in Shipley were ice-cream sellers and organ grinders. Unless of course it was Mr Settimo, the photographer. The mind boggles. Maybe Ma had had a Settimo fling. No, I was born *years* later. My black eyes must be telegony.'

'What's telegony?'

'Well I never!' Alice looked just like Molly for a moment. Molly's glint. 'And all your brains! You ought to do crosswords. Telegony is when sexual intercourse produces offspring who look like a previous impregnator.'

'That's not possible.'

'Of course not. Yet farmers believe it. It happens to sheep and cattle. And Crufts won't look at a bitch that's been out with a mongrel, even if there's been no issue. Royalty feels the same, come to that. Telegony is the belief that the female can be changed metabolically by a particular lover.'

'That's rubbish. Ridiculous. Necromancy.'

'I know. Yet why are we in Cremona? It's not on the tourist beat for a tiny ten-day Italian holiday.'

'We're here partly, I thought, to visit your Grandmother Ironside's grave with your granddaughter who's arriving any minute. And it's a month after your own mother's funeral. And Cremona must have been a refrain in your family for years. Almost in your genes.'

'Exactly. Metaphorical telegony.'

'Oh, Alice, what cock! Everyone looks up family graves. It's ancient custom. A taste people have.'

'I wonder if it will be Avril's? She's probably furious with me for dragging her here when we could have met her in Venice.'

'I don't think so, Alice. New Zealanders never mind going places. They're like Scottish people. They mostly *are* Scottish people. What does she look like, your granddaughter? I hope she's not like Florrie Ironside.'

'I've not seen her in years. Her father, my ewe lamb, was dark, of course. Very. The mother – oh, I don't know. She comes from Dunedin. Anyway, Avril will be here any minute, dear thing. I left a note in the hotel to say where we would be.'

But Avril from Dunedin didn't show up as they sat in the piazza, and it was late evening before a lanky, delicate emu of a girl in long khaki shorts and a cowboy hat and bearing an enormous pack appeared before them in the restaurant of the hotel. Gently mannered, hesitant, she greeted the wrong woman as her grandmother before being redirected.

And she was certainly not telegonic Italian. Even metaphorically. She was yellow-haired, quiet and mild, and her thoughts were far away.

Yes, she'd come from Venice. She had been there for a week. Yes, she was travelling alone – well, sort of alone. There was someone she had come back to Italy to meet.

Well, had expected to meet; but just at present he had not got in touch. She'd left messages behind in Venice. Yes, an Italian (the freckly Scottish skin blazed). She had met him when she was in Italy two years ago. 'But look – it doesn't matter. Grandma, could I have some of those bright fruit things in the jars?'

'Of course,' the waiter said and smiled, fishing down into the vast glass bell with tongs, breaking the spiral pattern within, holding out a tiny pear the size of her thumb, so transparent you could see through to its spine and brown-gold pips. Then a grape like a water drop, then an amethyst plum, a ruby currant. An apricot dipped in sunset.

She asked for more.

'Signorina, five is enough.'

She watched them glowing on the shiny white plate. 'So lovely. I'd like a photograph.

'Oh, help!' she cried. 'But they're *hot*! They are killing me. They are burning my throat. They are burning right down to my *heart*.'

'They are mustards, signorina. Beautiful mustards. They look so sweet but they are mustards. Very ancient.

"The mustards of Cremona." And see – you will find them only here.'

They laughed together, she and the waiter, as her blue eyes ran with tears. And then someone came to the table to say that there was a telephone call for the signorina, and she fled from the restaurant.

And her cup runneth over.

The next day was Sunday. The grave-seeking had been postponed. The granddaughter was not with the two elderly women. She had gone to the station to meet his train.

The two English women walked about in the spring sunshine and sat again in the Piazza Cathedrale. They listened to the great bells. They watched a priest free-wheeling out of the cathedral doors on a bicycle, feet in the air, grinning for Easter.

It was a fashionable, traditional day for weddings and at about eleven o'clock they began. Brides stood in the piazza at the centre of their attendant family groups, and each group was sucked, eddy by eddy, into the cathedral and each group emerged again with a foamy wedded bride.

Then each group stood for a moment uneasy in the sunlight after the darkness of the church, and from the crowd before them stepped out the photographers. They stood for an instant in charge of time, each one the conductor of an orchestra, a judge at tribunal, a general before battle. They cried out. They moved people to different positions. They demanded the buttoning of coats, the arrangement of hands, the carriage of heads.

'Look at her. Look at each other,' they cried. 'Now at me. Look at me. Look into each other's eyes. Now – kiss her hand. Exactly so.' Then back within the crowd they stepped, or paced impatiently in the square, awaiting their next victims.

Wedding after wedding after wedding, bride after bride, like puffs of foam, surrounded by bouquets of bridesmaids. Stiff egg-white dresses swung in the breeze, a veil suddenly flew up in the air like a pillar of salt. Wedding after wedding after wedding floated and chattered its way down the steps. Each bridal party floated and chattered, floated and chattered its way into the side streets of the city.

Now you can order superb titles directly from Abacus

☐	A Long Way From Verona	Jane Gardam	£6.99
☐	Black Faces, White Faces	Jane Gardam	£6.99
☐	Crusoe's Daughter	Jane Gardam	£6.99
☐	Faith Fox	Jane Gardam	£6.99
☐	God on the Rocks	Jane Gardam	£6.99
☐	Missing the Midnight	Jane Gardam	£6.99
☐	The Pangs of Love	Jane Gardam	£6.99
☐	The Queen of the Tambourine	Jane Gardam	£6.99
☐	Showing the Flag	Jane Gardam	£6.99
☐	The Sidmouth Letters	Jane Gardam	£6.99

Please allow for postage and packing: **Free UK delivery.**
Europe; add 25% of retail price; Rest of World; 45% of retail price.

To order any of the above or any other Abacus titles, please call our credit card orderline or fill in this coupon and send/fax it to:

Abacus, 250 Western Avenue, London, W3 6XZ, UK.
Fax 0181 324 5678   Telephone 0181 324 5517

☐ I enclose a UK bank cheque made payable to Abacus for £ ....

☐ Please charge £.............. to my Access, Visa, Delta, Switch Card No.

☐☐☐☐☐☐☐☐☐☐☐☐☐☐☐☐☐☐☐

Expiry Date ☐☐☐☐   Switch Issue No. ☐☐

NAME (Block letters please) ....

ADDRESS ....

....

....

Postcode ....Telephone ....

Signature ....

Please allow 28 days for delivery within the UK. Offer subject to price and availability.

Please do not send any further mailings from companies carefully selected by Abacus ☐